LISTENER IN THE DARK

An Old-Time Radio Mystery

by

Bret Jones

For information, email **Cozy Cat Press**,

cozycatpress@aol.com or visit our website at:

www.cozycatpress.com

COZY CAT
P R E S S

ISBN: 978-1-939816-25-2

Printed in the United States of America

Cover design by Laura Redmond

http://lauradawnsky.info

1 2 3 4 5 6 7 8 9 10

To…

The Ancient Radio Players

&

Stagestruck Audio Theatre

"Radio is a bag of mediocrity where little men with carbon minds wallow in sluice of their own making." Fred A. Allen

"The whole country was tied together by radio. We all experienced the same heroes and comedians and singers. They were giants." Woody Allen

LISTENER IN THE DARK
by
Bret Jones
PART ONE

RADIO GENTLEMEN: THE LIFE AND TIMES OF
TUCKER NILES
Episode #21

MUSIC: THEME.   WAGNER PIECE.

ANNOUNCER: KLMA in association with Hibler's
      Glass presents *Radio Gentlemen: The Life and*
      Times of Tucker Niles.

MUSIC: THEME BUILDS,   THEN OUT.

ANNOUNCER: Hibler's Glass brings you the finest
      glass for your vehicular, business, or home
      needs.

SFX: GLASS BREAKING.

ANNOUNCER: That sound means it's time for a visit
      to Hibler's. Glass with a guarantee to fulfill all
      of your glass needs.

MUSIC: THEME. SUBDUED/DARK.

ANNOUNCER: And now KLMA brings you the life
      of that not-so famous Old-Time Radio DJ,
      Tucker Niles…
SFX: SCREECHING TIRES AND CRASH.

ANNOUNCER: That man without a life and verging
      on total oblivion…it's Tucker Niles!

Chapter One

The heavy subdued theme music of *Suspense* echoed through the tiny chamber in the radio station. The Man in Black stated clearly, succinctly that next week Orson Welles would be the guest star in a new, mysterious radio play, so don't forget and tune in. Hands on the control board flipped a switch, punched a computer screen, and moved a slider for a commercial for Hibler's Glass to play rambunctiously in the foreground of listeners' radios. If they could hear the background noise, they would have heard a tired and grouchy DJ getting ready to sign off from his regular Sunday night vigil at the board.

Weary eyes blinked under the blue glow of the computer terminal that lined up the next six hours of programming for the station. A series of commercials programmed, followed by an even longer list of song titles and the computer sat ready to belch out the stale and inhuman commands to play at the appropriate time what had been punched into it.

"Silly thing," Tucker Niles muttered to empty shadows in the booth.

The commercial promised high-quality glass and service with a smile, which every ad seemed to have attached to it for some odd reason. Tucker slid the lever down and potted the microphone up on channel one.

"And this is Tucker Niles signing off for KLMA's weekly presentation of *The Golden Age of Yesteryear*, letting you listen to what radio used to—and still should—sound like. Next week we have a special line-up with *Fred Allen, Dimension X, Black Museum*, and for you old-time radio connoisseurs out there, *Quiet Please*. Our thanks to Hibler's Glass for their fantastic sponsorship and love for old-time radio and to all you fans out there who keep this show going week to week. This is Tucker saying good night from the Llama. See you next week…and keep the radio dial glowing."

He took channel one out and kicked the computer off into its pre-programmed journey of soulless, mindless radio. With a last loving touch on the control board, Tucker moved to the door and shut the lights off, bringing loneliness to the booth. He shut the door behind him and wandered back to his office to grab his satchel with his pack of cigarettes, schedule for next week plus shows on CD, and his newest issue of *Silver Knob*, the old-time radio newsletter he subscribed to.

The darkness of Sunday nights at the station brought him the happiness he missed the rest of the week. KLMA had been good enough to let him start this show two years ago not thinking it would fly. It did and he cherished his weekly watch at "the Llama." The rest of the week he jockeyed a regular slot in the late afternoons during drive time. He spun the music and plugged the products, but it didn't mean that much to him. He longed for sitting in the saddle on Sunday night.

"Good night, lady," he said to the place as he left for the night.

He lit up a Camel and blew smoke carelessly into the air. The smoke burned the back of his throat, but felt as comfortable as an old friend. With all the anti-smoking legislation and propaganda, Tucker had entered a dying minority when he lit up for the first time five years ago.

He unlocked his car, flopped in, and jammed the key into the ignition. Another long, tired night with the glowing dial as his only companion. Somehow it seemed adventuresome in some way.

"Hey, what's up?" a voice from the back seat growled.

Tucker yelled loud enough to shake the glass. The smoke in his lungs ripped out sending him into a fit of coughing and gagging.

"Hey, settle down, Tucker; you look like you're about to die," the voice said.

"Bobby?"

"The one and the only."

"What are you doing in my car?" He rolled down the window to fling the cigarette out.

"What am I always doing in your car?" He flung himself into the front seat and pushed a tape into the player.

"What now? Another *Lum and Abner*? I have everything that's available. And, over a thousand shows is enough."

Bobby sniffed, trying to cough down a giggle. "Right. As much as I love the boys from Pine Ridge, you should know me by now. I would never raid your car late on Sunday night if it weren't something hard to find."

Tucker pulled out of the parking lot with a last, longing look toward the station.

"It'll be there tomorrow, man," Bobby said, sensing his mood. "You have got to hear this. I picked up from a trader in Nebraska."

"Oh, great, your infamous connection in Nebraska," Tucker said, resenting the fact that Bobby had never shared his trader source in the cornhusker state for hard to find radio shows.

"Yes, my infamous contact. Have a listen." He twisted the knob on the player and waited to adjust the volume level. The fuzz of an ancient recording filled the air. Tucker could almost picture the needle scratching the groove in the ET from a long ago day and age.

"What is it?" he asked.

"Just listen."

Tucker pulled onto Main Street amazed at the complete lack of activity, but he knew he shouldn't be too surprised with it being Sunday night in Lyle, Oklahoma. The church folks had buttoned it up for the night with the weekly services and hitting the open restaurants afterwards. Tomorrow meant school, so the streets were empty.

The opening sequence blasted through the speakers, music blaring enough to ring the ears. Bobby moved the knob to a more tolerable level with a greasy grin on his face.

"Soak it up, pal."

The song didn't ring a bell for Tucker, but something about it scratched at a memory. He strained at any sounds behind the music, but it didn't reveal anything. Bobby stared at him with glee. Tucker knew he had only a few seconds to identify the show before Bobby claimed victory.

"Don't tell me," Tucker begged.

"I'll give it a couple more seconds."

Tucker strained harder at it, but couldn't place the show to save his life. He knew the announcer would open his vocal cords at any moment and that he didn't stand a chance at guessing it.

"The *Black Ghost*, man, come on," Bobby taunted him.

It clicked, finally, but too late. "Right, right," Tucker said, mad that he had missed it. Bobby had done this to him on many occasions. He'd only beaten him twice, including this one with the *Black Ghost*. He racked his brain for the particulars on the show's history, but could only come up with some rare program that had been tried out in the early 1930s. That's all he knew about it.

"Sit back and soak up that sound, man," Bobby said in his dreamy, sing-song fashion that he adopted when he absorbed himself into a radio program from the past. Tucker knew his own love for it would never match Bobby's.

"You get the hardest to find stuff. You know that?" Tucker asked.

"Aw, man, this is already out on a couple of websites already. You're behind."

They drove on in fascination as the episode of the *Black Ghost* pounded wearily through the speakers. The recording had something to be desired with some of the sound effects being inaudible and a couple of the voices disappearing into a haze of fuzz and static.

Tucker mindlessly wandered the streets, turning down each avenue that fancied him. They weren't going anywhere. Why bother? His imagination took over as he snuggled deeper into the folds of the story that barreled through the car's sound system. The movie in his brain flashed dark images that were fueled by the story—the voices, music, and sound effects that blended into a tapestry of film created by the juices in his own mind. He loved it.

There remained a saying amongst Old Time Radio collectors: "*OTR is like sex. When it's good, it's really good. When it's bad, it's still pretty good!*" Tucker's moralistic stance in life kept him from repeating it, but he did smile from time to time when it passed around in his thoughts.

And granted, the show couldn't be called "good" by any stretch of the imagination, but somehow, riding around with another fan of the medium in the blackened night made it feel right, honest, and pure. OTR fans couldn't explain their reaction to shows from eras gone by. While others—TV and movie zombies—bombarded themselves with countless hours of hopeless and witless shows, old-time radio collectors dreamed of an age dead and gone.

The tape came to the end. They rode in silence for a couple of minutes, still mesmerized by it.

"Wow," Tucker whispered.

"Yeah. I know."

"What a crappy show."

Bobby laughed. "Yes, indeedy, but hey, it still rocked."

Tucker joined in the laughter. "That's right. It still rocked." He pulled onto Bobby's street searching for the driveway with the familiar beat-up Monte Carlo parked hidden in the night. "You know something, Bobby? I'm beginning to think that you should be running the show at the radio station."

Bobby hadn't expected that from his friend and slapped him on the leg playfully. "No way, man, you give us a light in the dark. That's what you do."

"What were you doing out tonight, anyway?"

He shrugged. "I wanted you to hear the show I'd found. And anyway, the station is only a few blocks away."

"I understand all that," Tucker said. He felt one of Bobby's "mysterious episodes" about to take over. Bobby had been known to disappear for days without telling anyone where he'd gone or why. "What were you doing out wandering around this time of night?"

"Aw, you know me."

Tucker nodded readily in agreement to that. "That's why I'm asking."

"Had to think."

He knew what that meant. "You about to take off again?"

Bobby smiled that enigmatic grin that had become a trademark to Tucker. "The great Tucker Niles, Lyle's Greatest Detective on the case of the Missing OTR Bandit."

Tucker refused to laugh even though Bobby forced a fit of giggles. Tucker stopped the car and shoved it into Park.

"I know you well enough to think that you came by to say 'see ya' in your own way," Tucker said.

Bobby ignored this and with an eerie twist of his head stared blankly at his car sitting lonely in his drive. In some OTR circles, Bobby's addiction had been labeled a disease. He had uncanny knowledge of times, places, and shows that no one else had. At conventions around the country he had carved out a reputation for himself as someone who corrected the presenters, including some of the actors and producers from the golden age itself. Tucker tried to pry into his world, but had failed. Their friendship centered on their common love, but Tucker's filled his life, while Bobby needed the next "hit."

"Where are you going to this time?" Tucker asked.

"Have you ever read anything about the Holy Grail?" Bobby said out of the blue.

"You mean the Holy Grail, cup of Christ, and all that?"

"Yeah. Have you?"

"Some. Why?"

Bobby twisted back around with a new glow filling his eyes. "It doesn't exist, you know. It's just a story."

Tucker didn't like this line of dialogue at all. "Okay."

"Not the way they think, anyway. There are other holy grails out there. Some that people would die for...kill for."

Tucker desperately wanted to ask him point blank what in the world he was talking about, but somehow he didn't dare. Bobby, trance-like, stared straight through him and out of the car into the night sky and into the cosmos. His faraway glare only deepened the riddle into his friend's shielded mind—and life.

"Okay," Tucker repeated.

Bobby opened his mouth for another hail of mysterious words, but thought better of it. He pushed the door open, breathed in the sweet air, and whistled through his teeth.

"What about your tape?" Tucker asked, holding the cassette up to him.

"Keep it."

"Uh, Bobby?" Tucker began, but couldn't seem to find the phrase to finish the sentence. What had he been on about? And why the late night drive? The rare show?

"I know, I know, man," Bobby said, admitting to his weird behavior. "I make no sense half the time, even to myself. Just mark it off to midnight mumblings of a freak." He snapped is fingers. "Another great show, huh? The Midnight Mumbler with his side-kick, the Freak."

"I suppose that would be me, huh?" Tucker asked. Bobby's strange mood returned in his carriage and deepened on his face.

"No way, man. Not you. I'm both of 'em. The mumbler and the freak. I'll talk to ya later, man."

The door shut before Tucker could push the issue, if there had been any to begin with. Bobby Ross had, yet again, left more questions than answers to his strange meanderings. Tucker watched him tromp up to his front door, dig for keys in his pocket, and disappear into his house. No lights shot to life and he imagined Bobby simply collapsing onto his couch to get his night's rest.

What was the answer to his friend's strangeness this time?

"Only The Shadow knows," he said, mimicking the famous laugh from the OTR powerhouse.

The darkness unfolded around him as he sped off toward home.

Chapter Two

The inside of the house lay dark like an empty tomb from *Inner Sanctum* or *Lights Out!* as Tucker fumbled to find the corner lamp in his living room. He loved those two radio classics and thought of them every time he entered his home after midnight. The light flicked to life with a twist of the knob on its neck. Tucker settled into his easy chair next to it. Instead of grabbing the TV remote, which couldn't be found anyway, he flipped on his stereo set up next to his favorite recliner.

The gloom of the house soon filled with nostalgia of a *Jack Benny Program* with Don Wilson introducing the famous radio star. He shifted his feet up and pulled hard on the lever to release the foot rest. The shoes were off with a shove from his toes. Relaxation soon followed as he closed his eyes and let the bantering of Rochester, Phil, Mary, and Dennis fill his ears. He could see them all in front of his mind's eye playfully badgering one another behind large microphones partially covering their faces. He chuckled with the jokes and let his mind drift.

He shelved Bobby for another day. He knew that his pal's weirdness could only pull him down into assumption, resulting in a waste of time and energy. Better to let it rest until Bobby gets back from wherever he's going.

The blur of the night enfolded him as he fell deeper into sleep. His last thoughts were of a dark and rain-soaked strip of highway. Angels seemed to be flying or floating above an oily spot on the road. A car zoomed by, skidded on the asphalt, and flipped over and over careening into a ditch. Glass busted into a thousand tiny fragments. Gas spilled recklessly onto the road and flowed into the ravine.

Tucker moaned something unintelligible as sleep took him further down and away from the room, his house, and into the world of phantom shadows, aged pranksters, voluptuous women…and dead wives.

The spray of water from the shower shot heat into his face. He needed it. His body groaned from the sleep—or lack thereof—he got during the night. The dreams were lost like the rays of bright orange sunshine of the dawn. Rain clouds had replaced the sun and were preparing to unleash streaks of lightning and precipitation onto the earth.

Precipitation! The word folded out of his mouth with ease. The early days of radio had seen Tucker announcing the traffic and weather reports. He had come to loathe them both, but at least he worked in the field he'd been trained for. He let the water rinse away all memories of the past with a final clinging smirk to precipitation.

Breakfast took no effort and less time than usual. Cooking for one did that. He popped the bread in the toaster, poured a cup of coffee from the maker with the timer, and retrieved the Lyle paper from his front step.

The thunder rumbled across the sky shaking the windows in his house. The first drops of rain sprinkled onto his yard and front porch. He breathed in deep the cleanness it offered, praying it would rain the rest of the day.

In his office he logged in and double-clicked on the Internet icon. While his DSL fired up quick as the lightning from the storm, Tucker pulled on a pair of faded jeans and a black T-shirt. He blew at the coffee, waiting for it to cool down enough to drink.

His inbox had new messages. A couple from work updating him on news and local stuff he might want to mention in the afternoon during his shift. He had a few e-mails begging him to try their product to lengthen things on his body that had no business being longer in the first place. He deleted them without opening, disgusted with the junk that people sent out these days. There would never have been those offers in the old days on the air.

"Huh," he mumbled as he clicked on a message from Bobby Ross. The subject read: "(none)."

The only text of the message read: "Watch."

Bobby had sent an attachment that Tucker knew to be a video file. Since Bobby had discovered technology he had absorbed every particle of it he could find. And one of his "great" purchases had been a camera for web casting and for recording messages for Tucker.

Tucker clicked the file waiting for the appropriate software to kick into gear and load the information for him to watch. He dared gulp down some of his java, wincing with pain at how hot it still was.

A window blipped open with a blue bar zipping across the bottom of it letting him know that the clip had loaded. He punched the volume up on the speakers as Bobby's face filled the screen.

"Hey, hey, radio man. My nocturnal outlook on the universe has kept me up—yet again." Bobby fell out of the shot momentarily. Tucker adjusted the volume again. Bobby sat back in his chair and moved the camera down some. "And here I am again." He laughed and made a face into the camera. "Okay, so I'm leaving town for a couple of days. I guess what I couldn't say last night is that I think I'm onto the big one—if you know what I mean." With that, he winked and laughed again. And then Bobby did something that Tucker knew he almost never did: he became sullen and extremely serious.

"I'm not exaggerating, Tucker. This has been a long time in the making. A long time. I know I can't overload your computer with some big file, so I just wanted to let you know that when I get back…things will be very different. Not just for me, but for everyone in old-time radio land." He opened his mouth again, but no words came out. "And if I don't come back…" He let the thought trail off without finishing it. He shrugged as if changing his mind and leaned toward the camera one final time. "This is Bobby Ross signing off."

The file ended leaving the screen blank.

"Bobby," Tucker moaned to himself, "why do you have to be so cryptic and weird all the time?" He ran the mouse over to click the video software off. He shut his e-mail off as well and let the computer go into "sleep" mode.

He didn't even dare contemplate what Bobby meant. Why bother? It could be a thousand different things. He equated him with the boy who cried wolf. This was Bobby's SOP—standard operating procedure. But he knew one thing: it could only mean that he'd come across some ETs somewhere that he had to have.

The coffee tasted bitter the further he got into the cup, so he dumped it in the sink of the bathroom. The rain pelted the window above the shower making him feel more isolated and alone than he already was.

Bobby liked his shows on mp3, or CD, or tape, but any true collector loved to find the original electronic transcription discs that were used during the golden era. Something about holding a piece of the actual past in your hands made it that much more valuable. Bobby had a collection that would boggle the mind. *Silver*

Knob had featured it in a couple of issues the past three years or so. Bobby and his precious OTR collection had been the envy of every major collector out there.

What had he found now?

With a couple of commercials to record and other office business to attend to, Tucker again shelved thoughts about Bobby. He would mull it over later. Bobby had a tendency for the melodramatic, so just better to wait and see what treasures he had found.

The Llama brimmed with noise of activity that went along with a number one radio station in a mid-sized town in Oklahoma. Ad dollars were hard fought to get, thus a score of salesmen (and women) spent the majority of their time on the phone or blasting through the doors to have a lunch date with a prospective client. No dough and no show, the manager said often.

Tucker grabbed his mail, nodded to familiar faces, and buried himself in the solace of his office. Few gave him much attention on this hectic Monday morn. The rain pelted in waves against the roof of the building adding to his isolation. The walls wrapped around him as he cocooned into his hobble in the station.

The mail left something to be desired. Hibler's Glass sent a thank you note about the old time radio show, but not much else worth keeping. Something about the noise and the blast of the rain mellowed him out. His chair squeaked as he spun around seeking something of interest. He would cut the commercials, grab lunch, and knock off until his drive time shift started. It just didn't feel right today for some reason.

The Holy Grail...

Yeah, right. What good would it do guessing at Bobby's latest departure? Not any, that's what.

"Hey, what's up this fine morning?" a female voice came floating from his door.

"What is that? 'This fine morning?' You sound like half the canned commercials we squeeze out of this place."

"And a fine morning too, Tucker," she said.

"Oh, all right, have it your own way. Come on in, Courtney. What's up?"

Courtney Cannon plopped into the chair opposite Tucker and leaned back as far as it would go. Courtney had the night shift at the station and had become a minor celebrity in the area. Her voice had a silky smooth texture to it that sounded sexy without being dirty on the air. The manager started her out on the early morning drive, but saw the wisdom in moving her to the evening to keep listeners tuned into the station. It paid off and Courtney pulled down fairly good money for the market size.

"I just wanted to say hi. I listened to *Yesteryear* last night. I enjoyed it."

"Thanks," Tucker said. Any hint of a compliment for his show made him blush and he spun sideways in his chair to hide his face.

A face poked in from the hallway.

"Courtney."

"Jackson," she replied. The air had turned icy and Tucker detected it. He couldn't blame her. Jackson Mulroy could be a royal pain. He knew it, too, and played it up to the hilt. He didn't have to worry much. His morning drive (that he'd taken over from Courtney) blew the other stations out of the water in ratings. The management thought he walked on water.

"Lunch, right?" he purred.

"Since when?" Courtney said.

"Since now. How's Clara's sound?"

She opened her mouth to say something, but Jackson had already blown out of the room. Tucker watched all of it with a ghost of a smile. He felt sorry for Courtney.

Her sexy voice, nice legs, and deep blue eyes had every Tom, Dick, and Harry at the Llama slobbering all over her. None of them cared about what she had done for the station. They just wondered what it might be like to get her in the sack.

"Well, I guess that fixes that, huh?" she asked. She shot up from her chair and stormed to the door.

"Fixes what?"

"I thought you might like to grab a bite. But Jackson has this idea about some kind of promotion...I don't know...something about us doing a joint broadcast somewhere in town."

"Oh." Tucker couldn't think of anything else to say. Had she said something about going out to lunch? He couldn't wrap his mind around it.

"Maybe next time. Okay, Tucker?"

"Yeah, sure," he mumbled. His mouth became dry and his voice came out in a crackle.

"I've got to go cut a couple of commercials. I'll catch ya later," she said. She swung out of the room with a whip of her head, which shook her golden curls gently behind her like some kind of cape.

"What was that about lunch?" he whispered. Was it a date she was looking for? A nice respite from all the goons that fell over each other to ask her out? And why should he care anyway?

He dug for his new edition of *Silver Knob* and made for the back door of the station. He bobbed heads at a couple of the salesman, tried to ignore Jackson's loud bragging echoing from the manager's office, and sped past the break room without a moment's hesitation. If he did, he might tackle another cup of coffee, which he couldn't use.

Tucker shoved the door open with his arm while he slipped the lighter from his pants' pocket. The first tug on the cigarette burned the back of his throat slightly, but the feeling passed. He took another drag and flipped through his newsletter.

The editor had written another call for collectors everywhere to pool their resources better and let each other know what was available out there. Too many collectors had been hoarding lately and not sharing some of their finds. Word had spread that some boneheads had gone to great lengths to protect their tapes and ETs from other collectors who merely wanted the chance to listen to a sliver of the past.

"Crazy," he said to himself.

"What is?"

He jerked as if someone had plugged him in like a set of Christmas lights. "Don't do that, Mose, you nearly made me wet myself."

"I wish you had. That'd be the best thing I'd seen all morning."

Tucker took another drag. He handed his pack over to Mose, who lit up. Moses Stanley ran a janitorial service in Lyle. The best, in fact, and most of the major businesses used him. Tucker and he had become fast friends five years ago. The times had been hard for Tucker and Mose stepped in and took most of the burden off of his shoulders. He'd even sent a cleaning crew to his house for weeks and months after the incident.

"Nice rain," Mose commented. They watched it fall in heavy downpours from the protection of the awning over the back entrance.

"I like it. Mornings like this have that romantic feel to them," Tucker said. He stomped his cigarette out and lit another one. It seemed like an afterthought. He didn't intend to smoke two, but something about the weather changed his mind. "But I can't help thinking...you know."

"I do," Mose replied. He smoked his cigarette in silence knowing that it would be better than opening his big mouth and offering some philosophical consolation that didn't mean very much.

"So what have you been up to?" Tucker said, breaking the quiet. They settled into the routine of touching base about work, Mose's family matters, and other tidbits of information. After their tongues were tired, Tucker went back to his office to get some work done. Memories and Bobby's veiled hints at something big clouded his mind for the rest of the morning.

The rain settled into a light drizzle by mid-afternoon. Tucker slid into the seat behind the console like a driver in a racecar. His love affair with radio had reached legendary proportions around the station. Management used it for all it was worth and encouraged it. Some of the others felt like Tucker zoned out to some other planet that only he could be on when he took the controls. The listeners around town loved his fondness for the airwaves, his joviality, and his flair for the melodramatic for comedic affect.

Courtney walked by the window and waved. He nodded and pulled the microphone closer to his mouth. The commercial faded out into sweet nothingness and he began his shift.

On his way home that afternoon he ran over the ads he had cut. He could be a stickler for perfection and he felt that maybe tomorrow he would record them again. One of them for Hibler's Glass he would definitely re-do. Because they sponsored the Sunday night old-time radio time, he had a soft spot for them and did everything in his power to make them happy. Over the last couple of years he and the owner had become close over their love of the old radio shows.

Dinner came easy for him–slid out of a packet and popped into the microwave. He resisted the urge to flip on the boob-tube and slipped in an mp3 of *Fibber McGee and Molly* instead. The signature laughter started the program for which it was known for and he trudged back into the kitchen to retrieve his culinary delicacy.

Fibber had decided to be a fix-it man around their house and Molly patiently waited for the whole thing to fall apart. It did as always, which was another trademark of the classic show. The two actors had been in vaudeville like the majority of the radio stars and worked their gig until they were discovered on the airwaves and became a national hit. Tucker loved the couple that lived on "Wistful Vista" and counted it as one of his all-time favorites.

The show slid into its spot for the advertisement for the sponsor, Johnson's Wax. Other collectors usually ignored the pleading and begging of the sponsors, but Tucker found it somehow appealing in comparison to all the modern-day salesmanship that blasted the radio waves.

He finished his dinner and threw the remnants into the trash. The show finished up with a burst of applause, to which he joined in, and he settled back into his favorite chair to listen to another. He didn't have much going that night–like most nights–and his only friend late in the evening rested in a golden glow from a dial.

The phone rang at his elbow.

"Hello?"

"Mr. Niles?"

"Yes."

"Lyle Police Department."

He shot up in the recliner and stopped the mp3 player. "Yes?"

"We have this number as a contact."

"Okay," he answered. "For who?" he asked.

"A neighbor of Bobby Ross gave it to us."

"Bobby?"

"Yes. Could you come over here, sir? We know Mr. Ross is out of town–according to his neighbor–and his house has been broken into."

Chapter Three

Phone calls at home still caused Tucker to jump. If he didn't need it so bad, he would have had it removed a long time ago. Some people are smell-oriented with their memories. A perfume, a piece of steak wafting about, or a whiff of potpourri and suddenly you were miles away. Tucker knew that sounds were his memory trigger. Even changing phones to another ringer hadn't eased his mind from its invading sound.

Grabbing some shoes by the door, he shot outside and into his car. He made the trip to Bobby's in nothing flat. For years he had warned Bobby about insuring his collection and other knickknacks, but his friend wouldn't hear of it. He convinced himself that only a few even knew the worth of what he possessed.

He hadn't stuck to OTR, either. He had old mags, ancient toys from an era dead and gone, and some G.I. Joes that wore worth a few thousand. Theft worried Tucker more than it did Bobby. No details had been disclosed over the phone, but Tucker imagined the absolute worst.

He killed the engine after he slid in behind a Lyle patrol car. Adam Stiles stood waving in the doorway. Stiles and Tucker knew each other casually from interviews for the station over the years. Primarily Lyle's homicide detective, Stiles acted as just about anything the medium-sized town needed in way of law enforcement.

"Hey, Tucker, glad you could make it," Stiles said as Tucker entered the house. A couple of policemen were scanning the place hoping for a clue, but everything appeared to be in its place.

"What's up, Officer Stiles?" Tucker asked.

"Just Adam," he replied. "A neighbor reported seeing something strange early this morning during the heaviest of the downpour earlier this afternoon. Didn't know what exactly, so we called around looking for Mr. Ross."

Tucker glanced around the living room. Nothing had been touched. Scores of shelves held valuable pieces of memorabilia. Dolls in original packaging, figurines, and even a Buck Rogers ray gun decorated the walls, but no damage or anything missing. Tucker felt he would know, too, as much as he had spent there.

"Is Bobby not around?" Tucker asked, feeling foolish for not knowing himself.

"His mother said he'd flown out of town early this morning."

Why hadn't Bobby said anything last night? Tucker asked himself. Had he made the video clip right before he left?

"Why don't you take a look around and see if anything's out of place," Stiles said. He waved around the living room. "As far as the naked eye can tell, nothing happened here."

"Is the next door neighbor sure it wasn't Bobby?" Tucker asked.

"She swears it wasn't. Said the guy was way too big for Mr. Ross."

"Great."

Tucker ambled through the place. He couldn't put a finger on it, but something about the house didn't seem right. So many collectibles, but no Bobby. Maybe that was it. These things of plastic, cloth, and metal seemed lifeless without the collector there to take care of them, to keep them clean, to love them. He shook the thought loose from his mind. It was too morbid. And for that matter, Bobby was gone on a trip, not gone for good.

But there was something...

Tucker touched the packaging on a couple of G.I. Joes that Bobby always bragged about. If someone had broken in, they had either a bad eye for collectibles, or were looking for something else. The Joes were worth a few thou by themselves. Tucker couldn't imagine anyone overlooking those.

But he assumed too much. Maybe this wasn't someone looking for snatchable collectibles. Maybe this was just an average, ordinary break-in.

Yeah, right. With nothing busted and nothing apparently missing? Tucker eased back to the bedrooms on the north side of the house. Stiles followed.

"We've tried reaching Mr. Ross, but his mother doesn't have a contact number for him."

"Yeah, he's not a cell phone fan. He owns one, but rarely turns it on. Loves the internet and his webcam, but hates cell phones with a purple passion. The reason she doesn't have the number is because Bobby doesn't know it."

"Wish I didn't need mine or I'd agree with him wholeheartedly," Stiles said. They shared a laugh over the bane of the cell phone industry. Tucker focused his attention to the back bedroom that held more of Bobby's stuff.

Bobby's three-bedroom house bulged at the seams with things he had collected over the years. His mother refused to come see him at his abode. She preferred to stay away from the pack-rat habits of her son. She loved him all right, but couldn't bear to stay in his house longer than five minutes before she felt the urge to straighten everything up. Bobby would cry foul and they would get into it over his incurable habit.

Tucker witnessed the arguments and wished he hadn't. They weren't pretty.

The smallest bedroom stored other of Bobby's hidden treasures. Tucker glanced through the piles of material to spot anything out of place. He didn't really know if he'd spot anything missing back here, but he gave it a shot anyway. Anything for his friend.

"This guy collects a lot of junk," Stiles commented to no one at all.

"Not junk, Officer Stiles, collectibles," Tucker said.

"Right. Sorry. I just couldn't ever get into this kind of thing."

Tucker chuckled. "Not even baseball cards?"

Stiles shrugged. "Sure, those."

Tucker pointed to a couple of boxes stacked in the corner. "Take a gander over there."

Stiles rummaged through a cardboard box crammed tight with baseball cards. He gaped in amazement.

"Holy cow," he muttered.

"Yep," Tucker said, "probably enough there for Bobby to live nicely for the rest of his life."

"Why doesn't he sell these? I'm sure he'd get a small fortune on eBay."

Tucker lifted the lid to another box and spotted a collection of vintage golden age comic books. He did a quick tally and whistled. Bobby hadn't shown him this stuff. This was enough to take a couple of years off from the radio station and travel the countryside with.

"He's a collector, Officer Stiles."

"Adam," Stiles corrected.

"Right. Anyway, he's not a seller. Bobby surrounds himself with pop culture because that's what he loves."

Stiles stopped perusing the baseball cards long enough to weigh that one over. "Why is that?"

"He just is. He can't bear to part with anything he's found. It really is a treasure to him. If something is out of place in this, he knows it and it infuriates him."

"Again, why?"

Tucker shrugged. How could he explain this to a non-collector? He had his own fetish with old-time radio to deal with, but Bobby had a desire to own a little bit of everything out there.

"He's a hoarder, Officer–Adam. He has this psychological condition that causes him to compulsively hoard."

Stiles snapped his fingers. He tossed the rest of the baseball cards back into the box. "I think I saw an episode of Dr. Phil that talked about that."

"Then you saw Bobby. That's him to a tee. He has a great job, but won't save any money, doesn't have a 401k plan, and isn't interested in stocks or bonds. His obsession is surrounding you."

"And someone would want to steal this?"

Tucker shut the lid on the comics. "I guess not. At least not that I can see. And believe me, they could've made off like bandits with just a couple of armloads of this stuff."

He and Stiles passed back into the hallway into the middle bedroom. This is where Bobby slept. A few of his choice items decorated his "palace of pleasure" as he dubbed it. Tucker thought it resembled a squirrel's nest. This room actually had order to it in comparison to the rest of the house. The computer sat on a stand across from the bed, which Bobby used as his desk chair. The computer was shut down.

"This is pathological," Stiles said.

"Yes, it is. It's part of his charm."

"But I still don't understand why, Mr. Niles."

"Tucker."

"Tucker," Stiles repeated, getting adjusted to the first-name basis.

Nothing looked out of the ordinary, so Tucker exited for the last bedroom on the other end of the hallway. Tucker and Bobby had dubbed this room the "treasure room" as it held the transcription discs that Bobby had bought over the years. He also had a player tucked back in there somewhere, but the real pearls were in the discs themselves. Bobby's collection represented thousands of hours of vintage radio broadcasts that the average Joe public had never been exposed to.

In neat stacks and rows of shelving rested hundreds of wax discs that had been etched by machinery recording the classic voices of old-time radio. From the labels stuck in the center of the discs, Tucker saw shows from *The Chase and Sanborn Hour*, which meant Edgar Bergen/Charlie McCarthy, *Light's Out!*, *The Jack Benny Program, The Easy Aces, Amos and Andy, The Shadow*, and hundreds more. Bobby's collection was a slice of the golden age of radio broadcasting. A style and type that would never see the airwaves again.

Tucker waxed nostalgic as he lightly touched the sleeves protecting the discs.

"Crazy," Stiles whispered.

"Beautiful. You asked why Bobby does this. It's right here in front of you. It's love. A passion for the past, not just to preserve it, but to enjoy it as it's supposed to be."

"You sound like one of the flock," Stiles said with a wiry grin.

"Yeah, I'm into this stuff, too. Well, not like this, but I love the old shows."

"*The Shadow*, stuff like that?"

"And so much more."

Stiles, afraid to touch anything, stayed by the door. Everything seemed to be in place. Every burglar leaves some kind of mess behind. If there had been a break-in, which he doubted now, there would have been some kind of evidence. Some kind of proof.

Quietly, Tucker hummed the *Lum and Abner* theme song that he loved so much. It was called *Evalina* and was the most popular with the fans. He had gone to the festival in Mena, Arkansas, the area where the actors were originally from. He'd had a ball. One of the transcription discs with their label sent his memory flying to it, embracing it.

And then he saw it.

"Wait a minute," he said.

"What is it?"

Tucker didn't answer immediately. He stepped forward as if toward a mine field. Unique in its clutter, this room Bobby had actually organized in type of show and then in alphabetical order in each category. Over in the far corner he had stacked his collection of adventure shows. Two of the discs were pulled a couple of inches out from the rest of them—something Bobby wouldn't allow in a million years.

"There," Tucker said pointing.

"What? All I see is more of these...what are they?"

"Transcription discs."

"Yeah, those. What is it?"

Tucker touched the paper sleeves on the discs. "These have been pulled out. And before you say something, Adam, Bobby would never have done this. This was his best-loved collection. He kept it clean and in order. Believe me."

Stiles joined Tucker. He touched the sleeves as well hoping they would spill the truth about who had been here—if anyone. He still had his doubts, but this DJ from the local radio station seemed so convinced. So convicted. He knew his friend and that's what Stiles trusted on many of his cases. Knowledge of loved one's movements, habits, and idiosyncrasies solved cases more often than not.

"These two?" Stiles asked.

"Yes. Those."

"What are they?"

Tucker pulled them from the stack to read the labels. He smiled. His favorite. Bobby's too, for that matter. *I Love a Mystery* by Carlton E. Morse. He let Stiles read the labels.

"I don't get it," he said.

Tucker slid them back into their slot. He let a finger hesitate on the sleeve of the one on top. "One of the favorites of the old-time radio fans out there."

"Really? How so?"

Tucker left the room, turning the light off after him. Stiles followed him back into the living room. Stiles dismissed the other policemen with a wave of his hand leaving him and Tucker alone in the house. It felt lonely and unguarded without Bobby there, Tucker thought.

"It's too long of a story," Tucker said, "but suffice it to say, folks out there love it and have since it first broadcast back in 1939. As a matter of fact, I'm playing a couple on my show the week after next. You ought to listen."

"I might just do that." Stiles rubbed a place on the carpet with his toe. "So that's it then? Nothing else appears to be out of place?"

"Nope. Just those two transcription discs." Tucker plopped down into one of the easy chairs facing the TV. "You know, Bobby may have pulled them out to catalogue them. I've been bugging him for ages now to put into a spreadsheet on his computer just exactly what he's got. Maybe he started."

"We'll ask him when we reach him," Stiles said. He took a card from his wallet and passed it over. "Call me if he gets in touch with you. I'm sure it's just routine now. Just a matter of filing the report. Right now it's no harm, no foul."

"I hope so. I really do."

Stiles strode to the door. "And maybe you could talk to his mother. She seemed all out of sorts about this."

"She would be. She's kind of a nervous person, especially with Bobby."

"Only child?"

"No. She lost Bobby's older brother in Iraq a few years back."

"Oh. Not good."

"Never is."

"We'll be out here filling out some of the details in the report if you'll just lock up behind you," Stiles said.

"Thanks. I appreciate it. And I know Bobby does."

"I just wish we could help more here."

Tucker shrugged. "Who knows? Maybe the lady across the street made a mistake. It happens."

"It does. Just let us know if he contacts you."

"I will."

Stiles left the house with the door standing open. Tucker measured everything out again as he glanced around the room. Not one thing appeared out of place. Not one item was gone.

So why did he feel a nervous knot in his gut?

The Holy Grail...

Bobby had left it hanging in classic Bobby style. Tucker could only guess and that never got him anywhere.

He got up from the chair. A last look brought only sadness. His friend the cavalier hoarder was out there somewhere on some secret find and here he was playing detective for a non-existent crime.

The things of vintage radio crime.

Chapter Four

The call to Bobby's cell phone failed. Tucker knew that he despised owning one, but had succumbed like the rest of the "mindless horde," as he dubbed society, but he almost never turned it on. He loved his computer with e-mail, instant messaging other old-time radio fans, and downloading his latest audio find to his hard drive.

"All right, Bobby," Tucker said through a yawn, "I'll zip you an e-mail in the morning then."

He wrapped up in an Indian blanket bought in New Mexico on a vacation from all those years ago. He smelled something close to happiness in its fibers. He enveloped himself in its cocoon as the opening chords of *The Amos and Andy Show* punched in the night air.

He didn't judge the white men playing blacks on the radio. The fact of the matter was it had been the most popular show of its kind during a long ago era. Of course modern culture would look back with cocked eyebrows and hateful tones. But who knew what the next generation would scoff at from his own time? He could care less. The show had humor, wit, and heart. He would let his belief be suspended and let the melody of the voices drift, helping him go to sleep.

Dreams came as they so often did with violence and flame. This time he saw things in black and white, but hearing the noises in booming stereophonic sound. Shattered glass glittered in creamy moonlight. Wetness spread with fire licking at its edges. A cacophony of sounds echoed through the dream. Sirens roared in the distance. A man's cries seared behind the snap of flames. Too many things to pinpoint at once. Too many nightmares that followed the same path...

He didn't jerk up as he often did. This time he rolled over off of the La-Z-Boy onto the floor. He'd gotten too hot. Sweat dripped onto the edge of his lip. Kicking the blanket off, Tucker stood up and carefully walked down the hallway to his bathroom.

The tile felt cold, which was nice. He drenched his face with lukewarm water. Not daring to look at himself in the mirror, he slapped out for a towel. He dried his forehead and down his nose. Stumbling to the toilet, he took a leak.

"Oh, man, that's the pits."

Tucker knew he shouldn't, but he decided to sleep in his bed for a change. He thrust himself under the covers and went back to sleep.

This time the noise and fire stayed away.

Tapping the keys as quickly as he could, Tucker typed out the message about Bobby's break-in. He hit the send button, made sure it blipped out into cyberspace, and stripped for a shower, the unpleasantness from just a few hours before nearly forgotten. Actually, the dream happened so often he simply took it in stride.

He crammed a granola bar down his throat with a scalding hot cup of coffee following. He needed work to calm his nerves. The voices on the air would work their magic. Being behind the control board, he could work the microphone and the sliders to actually be in control of the world that he understood, a world that he loved and needed. The world of the airwaves was a world that he could understand. It was something that he could comprehend. In its own ephemeral way, he could touch it, grasp and hold onto it.

He grabbed a hat out of the hall closet and locked the door behind him. He lit up the first smoke of the day and let his lungs absorb its nicotine filled smoke. Not liking the smoke to be in his car, he finished it outside in the dampness of the morning. The rain from the day before soaked the surrounding neighborhood. He loved the trees and the whispering wind to the wet leaves. It reminded him of the static that he heard on old-time radio recordings that had 1000 tiny little scratches that the needle picked up and transferred through the speakers.

If only he could disappear into the folds of the radio and live in those imaginative places created by writers, actors and sound technicians from so many years ago, he could be at peace. He stepped on the remainder of his smoldering cigarette, hopped into his car and drove off to work.

He stayed away from the rest of the staff at the station. His heart wasn't into small talk, or shoptalk for that matter. He buried himself in cutting commercials that he would use throughout his slots in the afternoon. Feeling more persnickety then he usually did, he re-recorded many of the spots over and over again until he was completely satisfied.

A knock came at the door, which he wanted to ignore, but with a sense of relief acknowledged. The hours spent on work actually made him hungry for some kind of human contact. He hoped it was Mose wanting to clear out the trash.

"Hey you, are you going to be in here all afternoon?" Courtney said. She sauntered in the room and sat down on a stool next to him looking over his work load. "How many of these things are you going to cut this afternoon, Tucker?"

"I lost track of time, really. Do you need to do some work in here? I can go take care of some things in my office if you need studio time."

She laughed that contagious, throaty laugh of hers that was so well known to the radio listeners. He could see why she was so popular in the area. She had a great sense of humor and used it on the radio. She always found interesting people from Lyle to come in and interview. And honestly, she played some of the best tracks during her shift. And even though Tucker wasn't much of a modern music fan, he could appreciate her dedication and determination to keep and to grow her audience.

"Any reason you're hitting it so hard today Tucker?" she asked. She looked at his log sheet to check to see just how many commercials he had recorded that afternoon.

"Oh, I had a lot to do and had a lot on my mind, you know."

She laughed again. They shared a quick moment to ease the tension of commercial radio with all of its demands, timeslots, advertising dollars, and other things that interfered with just being on the air behind the microphone talking to a faceless audience, but an audience nevertheless.

"I read a quick blurb on your friend Bobby...what's his name? Ross?"

Tucker could only nod his head. He knew he couldn't stop a news story from spreading, but he knew that Bobby would mind. He let it go.

"And nothing stolen?" she asked.

"Not that I could see. Who knows? It could have just been some kids in the neighborhood who did it on a dare. You never know about those things, not around here anyway. Lyle isn't really known for its serious crimes, but who knows."

"Is he not in town?"

"No. He's out on one of his hunting trips."

"Hunting trips?"

Tucker gathered up his copy off the soundboard along with his empty cup of coffee. "Yeah, I'll tell you about it sometime." He pushed away from the counter that held the recording equipment and gallantly waved his hand before it. "It's all yours. Have fun."

"Thanks, Tucker. You better hustle if you're going to catch the beginning of your shift."

He glanced at his watch and then at the wall clock. She was right. He had about 10 minutes to kill before he had to go jockey his shift. He attempted something that remotely resembled a smile, which evoked another throaty chuckle, and quietly shut the door behind him leaving her to it.

Jackson Mulroy passed them in the hallway, said something pithy and was on his way to wreak more sarcasm on unsuspecting co-workers. With his mind still stuck in the recording studio, Tucker barely acknowledged the remark. Sure, most people found Jackson completely annoying, but Tucker always tried to give everyone some slack, some leeway and waited to see if the noose tightened up or not.

He grabbed his pack of smokes and headed for the rear entrance to the place. This time he had his smoke break to himself. He wasn't thinking about his shift on the radio. He rarely did that, well, except for the Sunday night old-time radio slot. That took a lot of planning, time and attention—and even love. No, he would just sit in the saddle and play the songs plugging in a few humorous (hopefully) remarks along the way.

He hated the cigarette that he was sucking on. It made him feel self delusional as if he could really transport himself off of this earthly plane to somewhere else. Somewhere peaceful without break-ins and weird friends and other things that stressed him out and caused him to lose sleep at night. He analyzed everything too much anyway. Everyone that ever got close to him always told him that. He knew it. He understood it, but he just couldn't stop himself. He breathed in the last bit of smoke from the dying cigarette and held it into his lungs until he could stand the burn no longer. Even that he analyzed too much. Who needed to smoke? He never did. Not until...

"Oh, forget it, just forget it. Replaying it isn't going to help. You need to learn something new, Tucker."

His shift at the board went without a hitch. Sure, he had the same guy call three times requesting Van Halen, which he played obediently but apparently the caller had missed it. He pacified the man with an old Billy Squire tune.

With a half hour left to go on his shift, he checked his e-mail during a commercial break. He quickly zipped in the password and scrolled through the mountains of junk and spam. His eyes lit on a reply from Bobby. He double-clicked the line with Bobby's e-mail address. It read:

> You're kidding, right? Shouldn't wonder, though, huh? That's what happens when you're trailing the Grail. Am I right? I know, I know here I go with being cryptic again. Never fear. There's nothing there. Tell me you can make a quick trip this Saturday to Lincoln, as in Nebraska? A few fellow collectors and I are going to meet to look some stuff over. Call. I'll have the cell phone on—worthless thing!
>
> B.

He fired off a quick reply. Lincoln? On Saturday? He mentally ran through his calendar. Nothing, as usual. He could drive up to Oklahoma City Friday night, take a redeye and be there early Saturday morning.

"Wait a minute, Tucker, this is Bobby we're talking about here," he said not realizing he had gone on automatic pilot potting down the fading commercial while bringing his mike up to being live again.

He felt his face flush as he heard the words run off through the earphones strapped to his head. An ad man outside the studio heard him on the speaker near the door and gave him a sarcastic thumbs up.

He replied with a gritty smile and snapped back to it. Bobby and Lincoln and a bunch of other OTR weirdos—and he meant that in the most affectionate way, being one of them—all spelled something beyond just the complimentary "interesting." He punched another track to life as his mind studied the problem.

As soon as he finished his shift, he tried Bobby's cell. Naturally, there was no answer. He may have promised to have it on, but Tucker knew his buddy well enough to know that good intentions were all he had when it came to clicking his cell phone on.

"Talking to yourself on the air, Tuck?" Jackson asked. A moron couldn't have missed the molasses-thick bite in his voice.

"Yep, Jackson, you know me," Tucker said. He also despised being called "Tuck," but he never let on. One thing about bullies: he never let him see the frustration. Let them feel like they've won and they'll love you for life—eventually.

Jackson chuckled and clapped him on the back with the palm of his hand. He actually smiled with sincerity. "Happens to me too, man," he confided. "But don't let the boss-man know."

"Never." He endured another patronizing slap on the back and retreated to his office. He dialed from his landline Bobby's number. Still nothing. He let the receiver bang down.

He logged into his e-mail again. He typed:

Am calling but you're not there! It's called an on switch!

~Tucker

He thought about calling Bobby's mother, but then decided against it. If she had heard from him, fine, he might find out some info. If she hadn't, it would fuel her already over-active imagination that tended to jump when it came to her son.

Moments like this drove him crazy. He hated not being able to *do* something. He prided himself on being quick on his feet, his job demanded it, but he got edgy when in waiting mode. He hated waiting. Waiting for things to go his way, waiting for his time in the studio, waiting for the news that he knew would come...waiting was more than just a thorn in the flesh.

With nothing else to do, he closed up the office, running into Mose on his way out the door.

"Hey, Tucker, how goes it?"

"It goes."

"I think we're done with the rain. Could've used more, but you take what you can get. Know what I mean?"

"Yeah."

Mose knew better and eased himself into the room.

"Mose?" Tucker asked from the doorway.

"What's up, Tucker?" He scooped up the trash can and dumped the contents into a plastic bag.

Tucker shrugged his shoulders. "I don't know." He laughed. "I think I ought to ask you something and you tell me something profound and wise."

Mose laughed hysterically and sat on the corner of the desk. Tucker joined in with him.

"You've been working too hard," Mose said.

Tucker sobered up quick. "No, it's just that...well, I'm a nut, Mose, you know that."

Mose didn't answer. He merely nodded his head.

"I think I'm living in this show, and not TV, either."

"Yeah, one of your radio shows. I know."

Tucker acted like he hadn't heard him. "And there I am walking in and out of things without a clue as to what to do or say, just like Fibber McGee or Gildersleeve or...whoever. And there's always this character...you know, the next door neighbor or a friend from work who has all the answers. The go-to guy."

"And that would be me, is that it?" Mose asked.

"You have it so together."

"Looks can be deceiving."

Tucker looked at him and caught his wiry grin at the corner of his mouth. He knew that Mose was trying for self-deprecation, but he saw through the act. Moses did have it together. And it wasn't just being one of the most successful businessmen in Lyle, either. His eyes showed the mileage and hard-earned wisdom.

"I think you're tiring yourself out on it," Mose said with the grin dropping. "You move in and out of things in life because you're tired of being connected. You'd rather live in some place brought to life in that imagination of yours. I understand that. We all do it. I do it. I daydream all the time. But you're going one step further, Tucker. You're needing to be there. That's what you're doing. You can't see the folks around you 'cos you're lost in some fictional place that never, and will never exist."

A quiet silence followed. Tucker nearly laughed with irony at it all. Mose had fulfilled the role he'd just described. The sadness crept up from his guts and he fought it back down as best he could.

Honesty could bite hard.

"Yeah, that's me, Mose, all over."

"There's gonna come a time when you've got to quit. And I'm not talking about your hobby, either."

"What are you talking about then?"

Mose frowned. "You know exactly what I'm talking about, Tucker. The moment you start feeling sorry for yourself, you are done for."

Tucker wanted to retort with something bitter and harsh like: "you don't understand" or "how would you know?" or "why me?" He didn't, though. He let them all go unspoken. He chased them all away.

He let the door slide in his fingers as he pulled it behind him. "Thanks, Mose."

"Don't thank me," he heard from a distance.

The noodles tasted flat, almost dead. He'd actually spent the time and energy to create a meal worth eating beyond just spitting out an order at the drive-through down at the end of Main. He couldn't decide if his mood had soured his supper, or if the noodles really were off.

He dumped them down the sink into the disposal and let her rip. The grinding noise buzzed for a few seconds sending the remnants of his inedible meal to the depths of the sewers of Lyle.

Opening a can of crushed pineapple, he immersed himself into another world through the airwaves. This time he had a *Dragnet* playing through the stereo. Not one for police procedurals, he could see why so many loved this show. Friday and partner were interviewing a woman who may or may not have seen something pertinent to the case.

He poured half the can onto a bowl of ice cream he'd heaped up for himself. A handful of mixed nuts followed with a dash of chocolate and caramel on top just for fun.

He shoveled the first spoonful into his mouth when a bubble popped up on his laptop, which he had opened on the bar.

An e-mail from Bobby the bubble told him. He double-tapped his inbox icon. He read:

I'm calling you at 9, as in pm—sharp. Be there, I hope.

Later, B.

He checked the wall clock: 7:33. Okay, fine, more waiting.

He settled into his recliner in front of the stereo and finished his ice cream.

His eyes closed soon thereafter with the euphoria of the sugar rush. He drifted in and out of Joe Friday's case and eventually missed the solution as he had faded into sleep.

Nine o'clock came.

The call didn't.

Chapter Five

Wednesday, just barely, passed into existence without a sound. Tucker jerked erect not knowing where he was. He checked his watch. Not good. He checked his voice-mail and cell phone for messages. Nothing. And for the first time since this whole thing started with Bobby leaving early Monday morning, he felt spooked.

The break-in hadn't done it. He wrote that off as a prank or a thief who didn't want to cart around a bunch of G.I. Joes and other collectibles. The lack of contact frustrated him, sure, but that was Bobby. Not only was it his style, he didn't have an identity without it. The video clip had been classic Bobby, but now made him wonder. The kicker, though, was promising to call at a certain time and then not. That wasn't Bobby. If he gave a time, he stuck to it.

"Aw, man," Tucker mumbled to himself. He picked up the phone, but didn't know who to call. And just what did he think was going on anyway?

Okay, okay so he'd been listening to *Dragnet* when he conked out. That explained it.

"Go to bed," he ordered himself. He pried himself loose from the cushions of the recliner and walked down the hallway.

The tiny sound of broken glass from his utility room stopped him. All right, he imagined a lot of things. And yeah, Mose had him pegged, but that was real. His breath cut quick and froze in his lungs. A flush surged through him head to toe. He could feel his face get hot.

Slowly, he rotated on his heels. He had twenty feet or more to go to get to retrieve a phone. Another ten would get him through the door that connected the kitchen to the utility room where he kept his washer, dryer, ironing board, and other odds and ends. A French door with small panes of glass recessed into it acted as the back exit to the house. He loved to see the sun peeping through those panes and shining off dirty laundry in the morning. It made him remember. And for one brief moment, he pictured soft hands removing a wet load of laundry and stuffing it into the over-worked dryer. The sound of laughter that came with a thrown wet towel out of flirtatiousness echoed in his mind. Whispery hair that floated in the space all around her…

Another tinkle of glass jerked him out of his memory. The sound came clearer this time, more defined and perceivable. *Someone was breaking into the house.* If the intruder busted out a pane of the glass, he could reach in and have the back door open in just a matter of seconds.

Tucker couldn't pick his feet up from where he stood. He hated confrontation. He despised moments of stress. He abhorred stepping into the middle of something and needing to make a decision. The phone beckoned from its cradle on the kitchen counter. His mouth wouldn't open as he considered yelling or threatening some kind of defense for his home and castle.

A piece of busted glass hit the floor in the utility room. A foley artist on the old radio programs he listened to would be impressed with the sound. He envisioned a sound effects guy on the other side of the door playing a horrible joke on him.

He heard another piece hit the floor. This one smaller by the sound of it.

The color drained from his face. His gut twisted cold inside him. A rush of goose bumps spread over his arms. All the signs of his stress level pegging out.

No time, no time…

His mind muttered the mantra over and over again. Being burglarized was bad enough, but to see the perpetrator set his teeth on edge.

He could hear the lock on the knob being fiddled with.

His instincts taking over, he dove across the counter for the phone. Plates, saucers, and other dirty dishes spread like the Red Sea and splashed into a thousand fragments on the kitchen floor. The phone slipped out of his fingers and bopped on the floor. It slid near the fridge.

Tucker, in one fluid motion, flew off the counter, retrieved the phone, and dialed 9-1-1. Nearing panic, he waited for the dispatcher to pick up the line.

"Hello, Lyle 9-1-1 service. How can I be of assistance?" the voice calmly spoke.

He projected loudly: "My house is being broken into. Right now!"

As the dispatcher walked through the steps of response, Tucker heard two things: a last tiny piece of glass falling on his utility room floor and the far away distant sound of retreating footsteps.

"Do you work all the time?" Tucker asked Adam Stiles, who sat comfortably at the kitchen table sipping a cup of coffee.

"Pretty much, yeah," Stiles said with a smile. Groggy, but still doing his job, Stiles had Tucker explain the events of that early morning for the second time. "You never know, Tucker, you might remember something you forgot the first time."

"You know, in *The Shadow*, Lamont Cranston would be tying things together and making some kind of conclusion about who's behind all this," Tucker said.

"You mean: 'who knows what evil lurks in the hearts of men?'"

Tucker beamed. "Yeah. 'The Shadow knows.' I play *The Shadow* all the time."

Stiles finished the coffee and grinned. "Yeah, saw the movie."

"Oh."

"Just kidding. I've heard a few of them."

"One of my granddad's favorites. That's where I first got into radio, with him."

"And if only," Stiles added, apparently not paying attention.

"What's that?"

"Just, I wish we could be putting things together and making some conclusions. A simple clue would be nice."

"Nothing?"

Stiles shook in the negative. "Na-da. Whoever the guy was, or gal, they avoided the mud and stuck to the sidewalks. We assume that because no footprints were found anywhere outside your house."

"Smart guy, huh?" Tucker was beside himself with confusion and fear.

"Yes, I think so." He put the coffee mug in the sink and ran some water into it. "He could have made a mess with your door, but didn't. It looks like the perp took a tool of some kind and tapped on the glass until it broke. The pieces were right below your door and not shot out all over your utility room."

Tucker frowned hard and sat in the chair vacated by the police detective. "Uh, what exactly does that mean?"

"Don't know yet. Could mean a lot of things. The main thing is he didn't get in. You stayed cool and did the right thing."

"I wish."

"You did. And I can see on your face that you're wondering what I'm wondering," Stiles said, taking the seat across from Tucker.

"What's that?"

"Is this tied in with the break-in at your buddy's?"

Tucker shook his head. "It had occurred to me."

"Me, too." Stiles thumbed through a couple pages of notes. "And still nothing on your end of it?"

"How do mean?" Tucker asked. Stiles opened his mouth to answer, but Tucker cut him off. "Do you mean have I come up with anything that someone out there would want bad enough to break into Bobby's house, apparently not find it, and then break into mine to see if I had it?"

"Very clever. But, yes." Tucker flicked over to a new page in his notepad. "That thought keeps coming back to me. So, nothing?"

"Nothing. I would want to think that the two aren't related. That it's just a string of burglaries going on in town." Tucker looked for reassurance, but didn't get any.

"Bobby's break-in was the first reported in a couple of months. And now you're number two. Two break-ins, well, one and then an attempted one in just under a week? No way, something's up." He jotted down a thought onto the page.

Tucker sensed the direction of where this was headed. "Aw, I see, I see. You drink my coffee, play nice, but down underneath you're suspicious." He made a statement, not a question. He knew the answer. Stiles didn't lift his head up from making another notation.

"Is that it?" Tucker asked.

"Switch places with me and tell me what you see," Stiles ordered. He watched for Tucker's reaction. Tucker squeezed his face with his hands and pulled down as if he wanted all the bad things to be wrung out from his eyes, down his cheeks, and disappear below his chin. "See what I mean?" Stiles inquired of him.

"Yeah. Yeah, I think I do. And so, you believe I know but won't tell because it's something illegal, or embarrassing, or worse: it's both illegal and embarrassing. I report the break-in and hope you find the guy without finding out what a couple of geeks have hiding."

"Bull's eye. You get the prize." Stiles grabbed his mug from the sink and motioned the coffee maker. "How 'bout another cup?"

Tucker rolled his eyes. At least he understood things a little better now. "Why not? You might as well pour me one while you're at it."

Stiles did so with a wry grin spread from cheek bone to cheek bone. He toasted Tucker's mug with his own.

"You know it does make some kinda sense when you look at it," he muttered as he sipped. He grimaced at the heat of it and blew over the top of the mug.

Tucker retreated to the living room. He plopped down in his comfy chair, careful to spill any coffee on himself. He pulled the release on the footrest and watched as it shot forward underneath his legs.

"Have a seat," he offered. "If you're going to drill me, you might as well be comfortable."

"Sure." Stiles eased into the couch opposite. "Tell it a different way, Tucker."

"It's no use denying it, I guess," he said as Stiles perked up. "Bobby and I have been running guns to Guatemala for the past year and they've caught up with us." Stiles frowned and set his mug on the end table.

"You don't have to be sarcastic, you know."

"Oh, was I? Sorry." Tucker wasn't, of course, and they both knew it.

"So, your friend, Bobby Ross," he began as if the prosecuting attorney in a case. "He didn't have many friends around here."

"Except for me," Tucker said.

"Except for you."

Tucker smiled. "Ah, I get it."

"Tell me it's a coincidence, Tucker. Not that I'll go along with it, but you tell me it is."

"It's a coincidence," Tucker responded. They both heard his lack of confidence in the statement.

"And then there's the fact that Bobby is gone. No one's heard from him."

Tucker, nearly spilled his coffee trying to answer. "I've been calling." He neglected to inform Stiles of the e-mail he received beckoning him to come to Lincoln.

"Me, too," Stiles said, holding out a black cell phone. Tucker didn't think many people had black cell phones these days. His was midnight blue with the beginning of *Suspense* as his ringtone. Stiles dialed a number and held it to his ear.

"I get your point, you know," Tucker mumbled.

"No one's there," Stiles said, closing the phone. "Thankfully his mother had the number written down somewhere."

"There are other collectors in town who know him, Stiles."

"It's Adam. C'mon, now, don't get all huffy on me. All I'm doing is following a natural cause-and-effect progression of events here." He sipped carefully from his mug. "Great coffee, by the way."

"Thanks. And there are others in town. There's a guy named Sean who collects G.I. Joes and I know that they talk every once in a while."

"Yeah, talked to him. He hasn't seen or heard from Bobby in a couple of weeks. And I talked to a guy named Ric from Sulphur. He's out of it, too. He doesn't collect the same stuff that Bobby does." All of it Stiles offered matter-of-factly, not accusing, but definitely in the know. He merely wanted Tucker to understand that he was no dummy.

"Okay, yeah, I don't see them messing around with him, much less me," Tucker admitted. "I really do not know."

"You don't?"

"I just said I didn't."

"I'm just asking, Tucker."

Tucker nearly slammed his mug down on the stereo. He pulled back at the last second before he made a mess. "Don't tell me something like: 'I'm just doing my job.' Okay? It's overused way too much."

"I wouldn't dream of it."

Tucker flipped the footrest back into its hiding spot and sat forward on the edge of his chair. "Certainly, in my heart of hearts, I want this to be a rash of burglaries breaking out here in town without any connection other than the fact that some slob wants more stuff. But Bobby and I are just a couple of guys who enjoy some of the same things. That's all there is to it that I can see. Sure, it's starting to look strange. It is for me, too. And I would love to play this whole thing out by saying something like: 'do you have a search warrant?' But you're more than welcome to search my house. In fact, I'll give you the grand tour."

"That's really not necessary, Tucker," Stiles said. Tucker's outburst embarrassed him. He hated putting good folks in the hot seat.

"Sure, it is. I insist. Come on."

Tucker bounced to his feet and motioned Stiles to follow. He did, but only to satisfy the growing anger Tucker displayed. He walked down the hallway drinking in all the images plastered from one end to the other. Tucker as a boy, a young man, behind the microphone at some radio station, another of him fishing, wedding pictures...

"Hey, I didn't know you were..." He let the thought trail off as Tucker disappeared into a bedroom at the end of the hall.

"My room. Take a look," Tucker commanded.

Stiles stood in the doorway with his arms folded. "This whole thing is really moot, Tucker. Even if there were something here, you wouldn't show me, and I couldn't do anything even if there was anything unless I had a search warrant."

"I'm trying to prove a point here," Tucker snapped back.

"I get it. I got it back on the couch."

Tucker waved at the bathroom tucked away in the corner of the bedroom. "Take a look. Don't crooks hide stuff in the tops of toilets or something? Go ahead, take a gander in there if you want to."

"I'd rather not."

"How about across the hall here in my study?" Tucker skipped across the hallway into the computer room. He threw his arms around almost like a conjurer on the stage. "You want to take my hard drive?" He felt his temper rising up inside of him. He hadn't experienced this much rage since...he refused to dwell on it. Not now, not while his fury sought a target to strike.

"Okay, Tucker, I get the point. You can stop now."

"No, I really don't think you do, Adam. I really don't." He swept past Stiles into the hallway passing a closed door, another bedroom, in fact. The door hadn't been opened in almost two years.

Stiles hung behind him slack-jawed and very tired. He'd pressed the buttons, all right, but didn't expect Tucker to lose it so completely.

"I'm not going to do this now, Tucker. Why don't you go sit down and cool off?"

Tucker whipped around ready for a comeback to spring out of his mouth, but nothing came. He raised a hand in anger, but he could only lean against the wall.

Stiles gestured toward the shut door. "Another bedroom or sewing room or something?" he asked. He half expected another tongue lashing, but Tucker just stood there transfixed on the floor.

"If it'll make you feel any better, you can go in there," he said hoarsely. He needed a drink of water, but the very thought of it made him nauseous. "I don't care anymore."

Stiles knew when enough was enough and he'd clearly crossed that threshold a long time ago. He carefully stepped by Tucker without making contact. Something deep lay within this man. He had an idea what. The story hadn't been told as he was still the new big city cop who decided to settle down with the wife and kids in the small town. He stood out as the interloper. But he'd heard the whispers. He had the urge to add something, but figured anything flying out of his mouth would be trivial, unimportant.

Tucker waited with a last shred of patience as Stiles gathered his jacket, notepad, and pen. With the sound of finality, an ending of sorts, the front door shut. He felt the vibration of it slamming home through the paneling on the wall. The purring of an engine crept into the house. He could hear it rolling across the gravel in his driveway. It faded off into the distance, around a corner of the street, and ceased to exist.

He didn't care to check the utility room as it was barred and shut up by the police. He did make sure the connecting door to the kitchen was shut up tight. A faint tear sprang up in his eye. He wiped it away before another one could follow. The fear of being ransacked and the interrogation by Stiles unwound him. Emotion this strong hadn't been felt in ages. He prided himself on control, but came close to losing it tonight. Stiffly he cleaned the remaining dishes in his sink. He laid them out on a towel to dry. With nothing left to do, and with no strength left to contemplate the situation, he plopped down on the couch and passed out in a matter of minutes.

In the bright, fresh light of the morning, he made the decision to call Bobby's mother, Denise. Once upon a time, Bobby gave him the number for emergency purposes. This counted as an emergency.

"Hello, Mrs. Ross?" Tucker said into the phone.

"Yes, speaking."

"Tucker Niles."

"Oh, yes, Tucker. It's Bobby, isn't it?" The tone spoke volumes. He imagined Bobby put his mother through the ringer his entire life with his dreams and eccentricities. From the first moment he met her he knew the strain they experienced with each other. He heard it now in her voice.

"Has he called you lately?" he asked, careful not to give anything away in his voice.

She laughed. "That boy hates phones, you know that."

"Has he called?"

He heard the hesitation from her end. He had.

"Uh, Tucker, I'm not sure about..." She let the thought fade.

"Look, I'll be real honest here, Mrs. Ross. Someone tried to get into my house last night with me here."

Silence ensued. Let her stew in it a minute, or however long it takes.

"I'm sorry to hear that, Tucker. I really am. My son is on one of his crusades again." She sounded more that bitter—almost in complete despair.

"Is he in Nebraska?" he asked, fishing.

"Yes, he was. But he called yesterday and said he was flying out somewhere else."

"Where?"

"He didn't say."

He refused to accept that. "Mrs. Ross, please."

"He didn't tell me, Tucker, that's the honest truth."

Tucker sat down in his easy chair. His fingers did a tap dance on top of his stereo system. He squeezed the phone closer to his ear with his shoulder.

"Mrs. Ross."

"Yes, I know, I know how it sounds. He refused to say where. He's onto something. Something very big, he said."

"The holy grail," he mumbled.

"Yes, that's what he called it. Another one of his lost treasures that he covets after so much. Where that boy gets all his money to buy all that stuff, I'll never know."

Tucker wanted to remind her it was paid for by his father's inheritance, but held his tongue. No use stirring her up anymore than she already was.

"Are you there, Tucker?" she asked.

"I'm here. Yeah. I just don't know what to say or ask. I'm just concerned, that's all," he said, hoping to keep her spirits up.

"What do you think I've been doing? I'm here popping green pills all day hoping to keep my heart from exploding in my chest."

"I shouldn't've called."

"Of course you should have. Listen, don't mind me. If he calls again, I'll make sure he gives you a buzz. Okay?"

"Okay. Yeah, that's fine. I 'preciate it."

"It's all right. And you do the same."

"Yes, absolutely, Mrs. Ross."

After more idle chitchat they rang off. He didn't know if he could keep his word on calling her if Bobby contacted him. He'd received the eerie e-mail the day before, but wanted to keep that to himself. The one fact he did have: Lincoln, Nebraska. Bobby protected his collector contacts as he liked to swoop in to some sweet deal on a collectible and show off for his pals—namely Tucker and folks out in cyberspace. But every time before he dropped a hint of what he hunted.

He shook the tangled thoughts from his brain and packed up for work. With a sidelong glance toward the connecting door to the utility room, he wondered if there might be another attempt while he worked that day.

"Oh, forget it," he said out loud. "If they find something, they can have it."

What do I care...

He cared plenty. That was the problem.

The front door lock tripped heavily into its slot with the sound of foreboding. He looked his house over as he slid into his car. It looked so empty, so alone.

Yep, what do I care...

Chapter Six

"Sorry to hear about your break-in last night, man," Jackson said from the opening into his office. For once, he actually sounded sincere, which Tucker didn't like.

"Thanks. They didn't get in, though. I was awake and called 9-1-1," Tucker shot back. This was the third person to offer him condolences on the near burglary. The Lyle paper had it on page two.

"What were they after do you think?" Jackson asked. He drank his morning cup from a KLMA "The Llama!" mug with annoying slurps. "You got any guns, jewelry, first editions, or any other stuff?"

Tucker shrugged. "None of the above." He gave off the vibe that he didn't want to discuss this, and especially not with Jackson, but the guy just didn't get it.

"Well, maybe it was some of that stuff you collect. You know, that radio junk of yours. I never catch the show Sunday night, but I hear it's really good." Tucker ground a molar or two, but tried to remain cheery and unaffected.

"One man's junk is another man's treasure, Jackson," was all he could say.

"Sure. I know. And I didn't mean junk as in, you know, junk, but is any of that stuff worth anything?"

"Nope, not really. And I didn't know you knew I collected old time radio shows." He heard the footsteps of Bulldog Drummond in his mind as the words left his mouth. Wishing this whole state of affairs could be a radio program, he envisioned Bulldog laying Jackson out cold with a punch to the face. He smiled.

"The whole gang around here knows, man," Jackson laughed. "You talk about it all the time."

"Oh, I do not."

"Ask anybody around here, Tucker. You're a little obsessed." Jackson slurped more coffee from his mug.

Tucker wanted to come back with some kind of zinger—Jack Benny style, but he kept his mouth shut. Okay, so maybe he talked about it some, but not as much as Jackson made it out. Surely not.

"Well, Jackson," he said, desperately wanting to shake him loose, "I've got a couple of Hibler Glass spots to cut for Sunday's show."

"Sure, man. I hope they catch the sucker and string him up," he said as he disappeared down the hall to bug someone else. He heard him yell for Courtney toward the other end of the radio station.

He couldn't face anyone else offering sympathy for a near-burglary, much less Courtney, so he snuck down the hall in the other direction. He locked himself into the recording studio, opened a file on the computer, labeled and dated it for Hibler Glass, punched a microphone to life, and zipped through the copy in front of him.

Without a music bed, it sounded flat, almost half-dead. Music laid underneath could add some pizzazz, but not much. He scrapped the take and did another. In thirty minutes he had cut the commercial twelve times, each recording worse than the one before it.

He punched the microphone off. The words on the copy blurred into a mass of squiggles and swirls. The headphones didn't feel right on his head. He took them off and set them to the side by the computer. He just sat there breathing. He couldn't muster the energy or strength to do much else. Okay, so he felt sorry for himself. Okay, so what? He brooded all the time anyway, so what did one more day matter in the whole scheme of things?

He needed/wanted a smoke.

He patted his pockets to make sure he had a pack and a lighter. With everything shut off, he exited and ran right into Courtney.

"There you are," she said. "You hiding out?"

He didn't know what to say.

She leaned against the wall. Her eyes were bright, always lit up. He wondered what kept them that way. She rolled those glowing eyes at him.

"I figured you were sick of everybody coming by and asking about what happened last night," she said. "Right?"

"Bingo."

"Well, you can just forget it," she answered with a smile, "I'm not going to ask. How 'bout that?"

"Thanks. I appreciate it." And he did. If he had to tell it one more time, he would lose it.

She noticed his edginess and the fiddling of his fingers. "You really oughta quit."

"What's that?"

"Don't play dumb. The smoking. It's bad for you. It's more than bad for you. Surely you don't do it for your on-air voice. Do you?"

"No, I don't."

"Good. You sound great without trying to muck it up with smoking. You'd feel a lot better."

"Yeah, you're probably right," he said.

Her face fell. "But not today, is that it?"

"Well, Courtney, I sort of..." He couldn't finish his thought. The look of consternation on her face stopped him cold. "I need to...I've gotta go...and then I've got to cut..."

"There isn't one reason good enough to want to punish yourself," she said. The clarity and force of it stunned Tucker. He respected her intuition, but she saw too far inside of him. "It's no good. Not in the end. It never is. You carry it every day and it's weighing you so far down you can hardly get up." She touched him on the elbow. "I see it every day, Tucker."

He tried for a chuckle, but only a dry cough came out. "I don't know what you're talking about."

She pulled her hand away like she'd been scalded. "You're too intelligent of a man to say something as foolish as that."

Her honesty nearly suffocated him. He took a couple steps backward just to get a breath of air. "I'm gonna go out back for a few minutes."

Her face broke into a smile of invitation. "After my shift some of us are going over to Roy's for some bar-b-cue. You oughta come with us. Get out of the house. Hang out with some of us."

He couldn't respond. Invitations to social events weren't a regular thing for him. And he sure couldn't remember eating at Roy's.

"Oh, uh, maybe," he said, retreating to the rear of the building and the security of his cigarettes.

He knew from the look on her face that she didn't believe him—not for a minute.

At home he buried himself into preparing a feast for one. Even though he wouldn't be joining his co-workers for dinner, he did have the inspiration to whip up some cuisine other than twisting the top off a can.

The stereo in the living room blared out a *Martin & Lewis*. Very few today knew that the dynamic comic duo had a radio show. He liked it. Very funny stuff. He enjoyed their movies, sure, but the routines that spit out on their radio show were golden. This episode had the boys doing a *Nanook the Schnook* routine. The sketch had a hilarious bit about rubbing noses.

Tucker checked his stir fry sizzling in his prized iron skillet. His mother handed it down to him before she passed away. It had been her mother's. Strange how physical items that surrounded him grounded him, made him remember.

He fought the regret of not accepting Courtney's invite to go out with the gang. He might have done it a couple of years ago, but the security blanket of his house and the voices on the airwaves brought him too much comfort. And he wasn't ready for the zone to be violated. He replayed the dialogue from earlier that afternoon between them, but this time he said the clever things he meant to say and she smiled with understanding. It didn't matter. He looked like an idiot because he was. He knew it with every fiber. Put a microphone in front of his face and he could rattle on *extempore*. But with real people, when it really counted, he could only flub and flounder.

He pushed the pan of rice off the burner to let it simmer. The chicken stir fry needed draining, but he could wait on that. He finished spooning in the sugar into the iced tea, dragged his spatula through it, and poured himself a glassful. While everything waited on the rice, he stepped back into his office to check the e-mail.

Throughout the day he attempted to reach Bobby. After his call to his mother, he figured she would too. Stiles probably dropped a few dimes in the slot during the day as well. So many trying to reach him, none succeeding.

Tucker booted the computer up. It hummed to life as it traveled through its routine of bringing programs to life. He clicked on the internet icon. The login and password slid off his fingers onto the keyboard in a matter of seconds, having established the routine thousands of times.

An e-mail from Bobby with an attachment rested snugly in his inbox.

It opened. No verbiage written in the body of the e-mail; however, the attachment was another video file. And from the MB size, a pretty big one. Thankfully, his e-mail account allowed for large attachments. He quickly clicked on it with the mouse. A box appeared asking if he wanted to open or save. He hit the open button.

Another box popped to life with a green bar showing the progress of the download. The seconds ticked away on the counter underneath. His video program came to life and there sat Bobby.

He scanned the room in the background, but couldn't figure out where he was. He couldn't tell when it was shot, either. From the date, time stamp it had been sent today at 4:32 that afternoon. The first few seconds passed in silence as Bobby focused the camera in front of him. He attempted a smile, but failed miserably. He looked haggard, tired, and somewhat bewildered.

"Hey, pal 'o mine," he began. A bit of his goofiness shone through, but only for a brief moment. The tilt of his head and quick glance of his eyes told Tucker someone else was in the room with him. Not shooting the video, but over to his right.

"Yeah, yeah, yeah. I know what you're going to say: 'why haven't you called?' I been busy, my man. Very busy." His nervousness came through in his face. He started picking the skin near his cuticles. Bobby stammered. And Bobby never stammered. He talked in circles, but he never struggled for something to say.

"Please tell me you're flying up here this weekend?" He paused as if he expected an answer. "You've gotta come up here. I've found something...I've found it,

man. What everyone would give their eye teeth for. I
have found it. If you fly up here—please say you are—
there's a guy that will pick you up at the airport. His
name is Dave Geiser and one of my collector buddies
up here."

Tucker frantically grabbed a pen and jotted the name
down. Bobby buzzed out the number. Tucker recorded
it on the paper.

What I have found…man, nobody in their right mind
is gonna believe it. I want to show you and Dave and
some other fans this weekend."

Tucker could see the marker on the video reaching
the end. Bobby had only recorded just a few more
seconds' worth of video. And it made Tucker lean
forward closer to the computer screen. He would replay
this part over and over again trying to make sense of it.

"And listen, Tucker, not a word, not a syllable.
Okay? You remember the story about the Holy Grail
and how everyone wanted it? Yeah. Same here. And
just like with the Holy Grail, there are people willing to
hurt you for it. So zip the lip. I know you will. See
ya."

He watched as Bobby leaned forward, not smiling
anymore, as he shut the camera off. In fact, Bobby
looked just plain grim. Someone willing to kill him for
whatever he'd found?

Tucker leaned back in his chair laughing. Bobby's
crazy sense of humor was crossing the line.

He replayed the video—and again the last few
seconds. He watched for every nuance, listened for
every change of inflection, and hoped for some hidden
meaning in the message. His prayer was that he could
decipher the jest in all of it.

He couldn't.

Bobby was serious, in earnest, as a matter of fact.

Tucker thought about forwarding it to Stiles, but changed his mind. Forget it. After the hidden accusation last night, this would put him in deeper with Lyle's finest.

What could Bobby have found?

All during dinner he mulled the question over in his mind. He didn't taste the food. His thoughts distracted him from enjoying, really enjoying, his meal. He didn't hear the zany tunes of Spike Jones and His City Slickers blaring from the stereo.

G.I. Joes? No, surely not. Tucker didn't care for the classic soldier figures. He'd be the last to call for that. What else?

Sure, his first thought had been of their common love of OTR, but what in the world was there out there that created so much intrigue? The hobby consisted of old-timers who missed the good ole days of radio and "new-timers" like himself, Bobby, and a host of others who really dug the entertainment of ages past. Okay, some collectors liked to find a lost show here and there and show off, but nothing life threatening.

The rest of the evening Tucker spent going through possibilities, still hoping that Bobby had played a tasteless practical joke on him.

Of course, he dreamed. There had been too much stimuli for there not to be. Fountains of water morphed into radios, not the new sleek models, but the classic Philco with the cathedral style face. Blurbs of noise that couldn't be deciphered peppered through the airwaves active in his dream-state. He saw himself walking below him as he floated effortlessly above observing the action. He watched as his dream-self trotted down the hallway of KLMA and into a 90s model Buick.

The one he used to own.

The view through the windshield resembled an IMAX theatre, large and overwhelming. The road spun beneath the car with the speed of a roller coaster. The curves barreled into view and spun him against the door panel. He'd been here, just not from this perspective.

Sound reverberated from the vehicle. It wasn't the loud muffler noise that everyone is accustomed to hearing. It resembled the odd tune that started *The Whistler* program that he loved so well and played at home at least once a week.

The dream throttled forward as the car jumped across the timing of the actual incident that plagued him daily. Shining lights from the car reflected off of the smooth asphalt highway. He knew where the curve was.

Afterwards, he'd driven it to prove something…he didn't know what.

And then suddenly he floated above the scene again. This time like the Man in Black from *Suspense* or Raymond from *Inner Sanctum*—he wasn't a part of the action, but a commentator, a judge.

He knew the curve…

He saw the wavy curls of her hair. The radio played something far off and distant. The hands rested at ten and two on the wheel.

He knew the curve…

She didn't.

As the car approached the inevitable, a vibration surrounded him, filled him. The air shook with it. The memory, turned dream, turned nightmare tore like fabric. In one fleeting instant, he transitioned from dream-life to reality with the shocking interference of a phone ringing.

"Hello," Tucker gasped into the receiver. His breath came in short spurts. He felt his heart galloping. Why exercise, he thought drily, just have a night terror, that'll do the trick…

"Tucker?"

The voice sounded a million miles away.

His first thought was Bobby, but he knew that was wrong.

"Tucker, this is Adam...Adam Stiles from LPD."

"Yeah, I know. What's wrong?" He didn't need Stiles' cold tone to let him know something was amiss, the phone call alone let him know something was not right with the universe.

"Bobby's been found, Tucker," the voice continued quietly, nearly non-existent.

"Where? Is he back?" He knew better. With the dream and it being the middle of the night, he didn't know what else to say.

"No. Lincoln."

"Lincoln?"

Stiles interrupted his thoughts: "From the way it was told to me, Bobby flew in from somewhere on a private plane, hopped a cab to a hotel near the airport, and got knifed walking up to this room."

"He...what?" Nothing computed. Bobby got stabbed? What?

"It was past two in the morning with no one roaming the halls, so he bled to death." Stiles reported it with deadpan precision, not wanting to invoke an emotional outburst. Tucker sensed it and appreciated it.

"You better come over."

PART TWO

RADIO GENTLEMEN: THE LIFE AND TIMES OF
TUCKER NILES
Episode #23

MUSIC: THEME. WAGNER PIECE.

ANNOUNCER: We return now to *Radio Gentlemen:*
The Life and Times of Tucker Niles.

MUSIC: THEME BUILDS, THEN OUT.

ANNOUNCER: The last we saw Tucker Niles, he had
lost a dear friend…who was responsible? No
one knew…but someone was to blame.

SFX: FOOTSTEPS ON CONCRETE.

ANNOUNCER: Could this be his last adventure?

MUSIC: THEME. SUBDUED/DARK.

SFX: GUN SHOTS.

SFX: A SCREAM!

ANNOUNCER: Join us find out…in today's episode
of *Tucker Niles*!

SFX: AN AIRPLANE TAKING OFF.

TUCKER: (voice over narration) My life would
have been different, but for two things: a car wreck and
the death of a dear friend. And now I had to reconcile
with one to follow up on the other…

Chapter Seven

The late night visit with Stiles had been enlightening for the police detective and not so much for Tucker. He sat in the dim light of his living room after he showed Stiles the strange video e-mail from Bobby and walked through the facts as he understood them to be. And no, he repeated often during the interview, he didn't have a clue what any of it was about.

The one thing the police in Lincoln did suspect: Bobby didn't see it coming. The layout of the hotel, the hallway, and the proximity to his room suggested someone walked out of a janitorial closet within twenty feet from Bobby's door and knifed him in the chest nicking the aorta.

No one heard anything—not a scream, not any struggling. The Lincoln Police theorized the murderer held Bobby's mouth until he died. There was some bruising around his lips.

At this point, Tucker begged not to know any more of the facts. He couldn't stomach any of it.

Stiles continued the macabre tale describing the search of Bobby's room. Nothing but a bag with clothes and toiletries was found. Bobby's wallet contained three hundred in cash, credit cards, and forms of identification. So, robbery was thrown out.

"So now what?" Stiles asked, waiting for Tucker's answer.

He couldn't give any. He didn't have any.

"Brutal," Stiles muttered as he made his way to the door. "No one there to help him."

"Yeah." Tucker couldn't come up with anything else but that. It sounded so empty, so cheap. Bobby was worth more than just a "yeah."

"Have you called his mother?" he managed to ask as Stiles hung by the front door.

"Yes. First thing before I called you." He fiddled with his notepad. He shoved his pen through the spiral of the wire holding it together. "And you really don't have a clue about any of this, Tucker?"

Tucker only frowned.

"Okay, okay. It's just baffling. This wasn't random and it certainly was personal. Shooting someone is ugly enough, but you have distance, or you can. A knife is next to them. In their personal space. Hearing them gasp for air." He saw Tucker's face flush and stopped. "Sorry. My mind works in the most horrible of ways."

"I understand. I'm sure I'll dream about it."

"I hope not."

"Me, too. He was…"

"What?"

"Oh, I don't know what to say," Tucker confessed. "He was…a part of my life. And I'm tired of people being a part of my life and then taken away."

Stiles remained silent as he watched Tucker fight against his own personal torment. He raised a hand to put on Tucker's shoulder, but thought better of it.

Tucker cleared his throat. "I just want you to know…" He couldn't finish the sentence. The shock and the early morning were too much for him to put together coherent sentences.

"Know what?"

"I'm going to fly to Lincoln."

Stiles shifted on his feet. Tucker knew he should've kept it to himself, but he didn't want to draw suspicion back on himself later. Stiles didn't have to say a word.

Tucker attempted that carefree smile of his, but it barely cracked across his face.

"I wouldn't advise that," Stiles commanded.

"Yeah. Me, either. But that's where he went. He invited me to fly up there for the weekend to see what he'd been up to and meet some of his other collector pals. I'm going."

A quick stare-down ensued with neither one winning. Tucker was going and Stiles wouldn't be convinced it was a good plan.

"It's a free country," Stiles muttered.

"It is at that." Tucker squeezed the door closed. "I'll call in," he added, mumbling to himself.

"Good."

Tucker made a pot of coffee. He added a couple extra scoops to wake him up. While it perked to life, he got online and booked a flight to Lincoln from Will Rogers World Airport that left later that afternoon. The flight stopped off in Denver for a connection to Lincoln; same thing on the way back. He didn't care. He just wanted to get there.

He dialed the number that Bobby left him for this Geiser guy. Not concerned about waking him up, he rang him anyway. The time was just after four in the morning. Yes, Geiser had gotten the word about Bobby's death. Being one of the last to see him alive, the Lincoln PD had already paid a visit, with more promised. No, he didn't know anything about what Bobby had been up to.

He rang off, not entirely sure that he'd heard the truth. Sure, with the death of his friend fresh on his mind and him willingly walking into a possible lion's den, he suspected anyone attached to Bobby. But something in Geiser's voice didn't ring completely honest.

With that out of the way, he made another phone call. This one to the GM of the station filling him in on the situation and his departure plans. He promised to come back to jockey his Sunday night slot. He vowed to himself to make it back for that. That night would be all Bobby's.

The coffee tasted bitter, but good. He grimaced as it slid down his throat and warmed his belly.

While he packed, he reflected. The busy work of getting a flight and getting packed bit back the emotion that now wanted to pour out. He walked outside onto his back porch and lit a smoke. Courtney was right, but at the moment he could have cared less. He planned on lighting another one after this one burned down to the filter.

What do you say, or think, about someone you knew, cared about even, when they die? Dying from any cause is bad enough, but by the hand of violence draws up different, stronger emotions from the well.

Bobby had been…what? A friend? Certainly, without doubt. A comrade-in-arms? Sure, if you counted the love of all things old as a fraternity of brethren bound by the unspoken word that what is older is sacred. He had been that, too.

Did he really know Bobby? Not really, no. Did he truly understand him as a person? Again, that would have to be a no.

He lit the next cigarette from the smoldering one in his mouth. The tobacco mingled with the coffee taste on his tongue and slid quickly into his lungs. The morning dew settled heavy around him, on his shoulders, in his hair. Birds brought to life by the first crack of the sun squawked and chirped to life.

Yet another day passing into existence as the life of someone he knew and cared for faded out. Time did that. It ate up the moments, the memories, and the feelings. Situations turned to sand. The world continued to spin. Another soul passed into the firmament.

He laughed to himself for sounding so Biblical, but for now it brought a bitter comfort. *All good things...* He hated the expression with a passion. They did and do, but he began to feel the balance of injustice swinging against him.

A wife and now a friend.

Too many thoughts sprang to life. A fragment popped into his mind of Bobby and his wife in the same room in his house laughing at Tucker for shushing them to pay close attention to a *Quiet, Please* episode. A cookout in some park came into view next.

Buns, relish, and sour kraut with a bunch of collectors with Bobby as host serving chili cheese dogs as they debated the influence of Jack Benny's humor.

All gone now. Nothing but slivers of moments all smashing together with other images of other days, happier times.

The sun burned a hot orange scorching the horizon with rays shaped like fingers scraping the sky. Tucker thought of a pool of spreading blood as he watched it grow into morning.

Bobby died like that, he thought. His life oozing out around him until there wasn't enough inside him to keep him alive. And the killer holding him down until he died.

This is not the best of ideas, Tuck...

But, nothing ever is.

He thought of Boston Blackie: *"Enemy to those who make him an enemy, friend to those who have no friends."* Tucker desired that kind of courage.

And in the coming days he prayed for it.

Chapter Eight

Tucker ignored the vibration of his cell phone. The phone identified the caller as Courtney Cannon. He couldn't handle any badgering about his feelings, so he left it alone. Others called earlier, but he ignored those as well. His mind drifted to other things.

As he powered the phone off, upon orders from the flight attendant in front of him, he cast his thoughts to darker things. It gave him a twisted sense of comfort.

Bobby died for...what?

He refused a random slayer. With nothing of his belongings touched, he knew the police in Lincoln didn't believe it, either. Answers would have to come from Lincoln first. Geiser would be the first point of contact and then, who knew?

Bobby had found his grail.

And the thing about grails is that there are others who want it, too. He played a dozen scenarios but none rang true. He just didn't have enough to digest to form a theory.

As his eyes adjusted to the interior lights of the plane, he pondered what idiocy prompted him to do this. An ordinary disc jockey flying off on a whim to dig for answers into the death of a friend? Hadn't he heard this storyline in some radio show? The details were different, but he recognized the situation.

He ached for a cigarette. He needed a swift kick...

The pilot mumbled something about takeoff, the light breezes to expect in Lincoln, and something unintelligible about moving about in the cabin.

He hoped the pretzels weren't too dry.

"Hey man, how ya doing?" the man calling himself Dave Geiser said. He took Tucker's suitcase with an easy flick of his wrist and they were off. "I'm out in front, which the airport po-po will just love."

"Po-po?" Tucker asked unsure if the slang up north would boggle his mind or not.

"The police. Coppers." Geiser flashed pearly whites as they trotted carefully through the automatic looping doors. The cool breeze washed over Tucker in steady waves.

"Ah, the po-po," he said trying his best to keep things light. They would get heavy soon enough. "I like 'coppers' better."

"Yeah, it's very *Gangbusters*, isn't it?"

"You a fan?"

Geiser slid the suitcase into the back seat of his Ford Escape. He punched a button on his key ring unlocking the doors. He motioned for Tucker to get into the passenger side.

"A very loud beginning, but a good show for old time radio," Geiser answered. "I don't get all philosophical like some of the geeks around here, but I enjoy it."

They eased into airport traffic to the main highway threading back into the heart of Lincoln. Unsure of what he could, or would, do Tucker eyed the scenery to keep his mind from getting bogged down.

"So by 'geeks' you mean other fans?" he asked. "Are there a lot of them up here?"

Geiser flicked a switch on the radio to some station where the DJ spoke what sounded like Chinese, or Japanese; Tucker sure didn't know the difference. Geiser lightly touched a button where a BTO song blared away. He left it there.

"Sure, yeah," he said, finally answering the question. He seemed disinterested or bored, or both. Tucker couldn't peg him. "Those who still like to trade cassettes or reel-to-reels meet every month to talk shop and sound pretentious."

Tucker found that funny and said so. "Just another thing for fandom to drone on endlessly about, am I right?"

"You're right. I got into it because my dad had some old tapes in the garage. I bought a reel-to-reel player from one of the stations in town and listened to what he had. I fell in love in an instant. But not with all the snootiness of it, you know? I like the medium and the stories, hokey or otherwise."

"I hear ya. We all have our faves, don't we?"

Geiser shot a glance in the rearview mirror, punched a hair more gas, and moved into the right lane. He gestured to an exit sign. "I live in Arnold Heights. When everybody gets off work, or whatever, they're going to come over and meet you."

"And talk about Bobby."

Geiser shook his head. "I'm assuming that's why you're here?" A careful sideways look to Tucker made him edgy, watched.

Bobby hadn't been a random killing. He died for what he chased. Tucker knew it in his bones. He could tell that Geiser shared the same thought.

"I'm here for Bobby, yeah," was all Tucker could say.

"He was on fire for something. He wouldn't say what, but you could tell he had found a big deal, which is saying something since there really isn't any cash in old-time radio, anyway."

"What was he looking for?"

Geiser laughed out loud. A crude, ugly chuckle, it grated Tucker's last nerve.

"You're asking me? Look, Niles, I met Bobby a couple of years ago at the Mid-Atlantic Nostalgia Convention. Everyone that knew him stayed out of his way because he got gold rush fever when he perused the aisles. You get me?" The sideways glance came at Tucker again.

"Yeah. He did that with all collectors, no matter what it was. G.I. Joes or baseball cards or just about anything."

"And he played it close to the vest so he could be the first one to show everybody else the gem he'd dug up. He worked the Cincinnati convention and a couple of others looking for things that no one knew about. He trumped I don't know how many guys with his knowledge of the past," Geiser said not hiding his contempt.

"That bother you?"

"You better believe it, brother. And listen, whatever third degree you're going to give me and everybody else, I'm just gonna tell you now, it doesn't bother me. Not one bit."

"Who said anything about third degree?" Tucker asked, almost insulted.

"Why come up here in the first place? The cops are investigating it. You've got nothing of his to pick up because he didn't have anything. You're here to find out what he was after."

"To find out what killed him."

"Same thing."

"I think so, yes."

Geiser swung the wheel to the right and the vehicle lunged forward onto an exit ramp. He quickly tapped the brakes for the red light. He clicked the blinker to turn right and waited for a break in traffic.

"I'm not going to lie. When Bobby got to talking about finding the ark of the covenant, I paid attention. And I wanted to beat him to it."

"I appreciate your honesty. He used the term 'holy grail' with me."

"Very Biblical, our Bobby," Geiser shot back.

"His mother is a good Southern Baptist, like nearly everyone from Lyle."

"Lyle? Is that where he's from?" The questions sounded so innocent, so devoid of any dishonesty, that Tucker nearly let it slide. Surely he knew where Bobby hailed from.

"You never sent him anything in the mail?" Tucker asked. He covered his caution with a smirk suggesting that Lyle was a small blip in the road.

"I never knew it had a post office," Geiser joked.

At that moment, Tucker felt like an amalgamation of a slew of OTR detectives: Nick Carter, Philip Marlowe, Sam Spade, and Johnny Dollar. If he could light up in Geiser's car, he would have. He examined closely Dave Geiser's tall, lanky frame with a Shaggy-like beard, dark sunglasses, and clipped haircut. Basil Rathbone's Sherlock Holmes would have better luck deducing about this man's life than Tucker. He closed his eyes to shake off the last effects of the flight.

"And here we are," Geiser said, pulling into a drive outside a neat, trim brick house. *"De casa de Geiser."*

When Tucker lay down on the bed that would be his for the next couple of nights, upon Geiser's insistence, he tried to answer the question thrown at him earlier. Why in the world was he here? Sure, in his imagination he talked tough, squinted hard, and carried a .38 that shot first and asked questions later. In every show he listened to he saw himself as the hero. He pictured himself getting the laughs along with Phil Harris and

Mary Livingstone, shooting the bad guys as Marlowe, or crooning the latest song as Crosby.

He turned on his cell and called Stiles back in Lyle.

"Hey, hey," the voice crackled in the earpiece. "You make it safe to the land of the cornhusker?"

"I did."

"Remember something you needed to tell me?" Stiles asked.

"Ever the optimist."

"I have to be in the business I'm in."

"Let me ask you something, Stiles."

"Fire away."

"What am I doing here, anyway?" he asked.

"That's something I've been pondering myself. My cop instincts tell me you know something that I don't."

"I can see why you'd think that. I don't, by the way."

"You're meeting some of his friends?"

"I don't know if you'd call them friends exactly. Collectors aren't exactly the chummiest with other collectors. Friendly, maybe, but not friends."

"Have you made a trip to see Lincoln's finest?" Stiles asked through a mouthful of something as the words were muffled.

"Should I?"

"What do you think?"

"Okay. That gives me something to do."

Geiser agreed to take him to the homicide offices of the LPD. He insisted that Tucker call him Dave as he drove through Holmes Park, showing a few sights along the way. Tucker did his best to pay attention. Lots of trees would be all he could remember later.

"I'll go pick up some stuff for tonight," he told Tucker. "One thing this bunch can do is eat." He kicked the Escape into gear and vanished into traffic.

Three explanations later to three different people and Tucker found a Detective Lisa Phelps behind a dirty desk eating an even dirtier looking sub sandwich. Fifteen minutes into the conversation and she still didn't know what he tried to tell her.

"This was a professional job, Mr. Niles," she said being careful not to reveal too much.

"What does that mean?"

"It means professional."

"I hear that in a lot of cop shows, and even in a lot of radio shows, but no one really defines what it means," he said.

"He was your friend?" she asked.

"Yes."

"And you flew all the way up here because he's your friend?"

"Something like that, yeah."

"Do I have to spell it out for you?" She wiped the desk calendar of any crumbs into the palm of her hand. She whisked them away into an overstuffed trash can. "I'd rather not."

"This is about the way he was killed, isn't it?"

She sighed as she wiped her mouth of any residue. Her middle-aged eyes carried heaviness that few in life ever have. He recognized it. He carried his own.

"Bobby Ross came in after midnight to his hotel," she said as if reporting it for the hundredth time, which it probably was. "Someone of undetermined height, weight, description came up behind him and slid a very sharp knife into Bobby. He bled quickly. Said killer held his nose and mouth tight so he wouldn't cry out. He put your friend on the floor. He put him there fast. We know this because of the blood pattern on the wall and floor. Nothing was taken. His room wasn't touched as far as we could tell. And there is no trace of the perpetrator anywhere in the hotel, or on any security camera." She took a deep breath to continue, but Tucker stopped her with a loud cough.

"I get it."

"You understand what I mean by professional now?"

"And this is a certainty?"

"Yeah, I'm certain about it. Why ask?"

"Nobody in the hotel saw anyone with blood on them?"

"You heard me describe everything. Did you hear me say anything like that?"

"No, ma'am."

"I'm not a ma'am, Mr. Tucker. I haven't been in years."

"Could it have been a lucky cut by the killer?" he asked.

"I wish. It'd make the hunt for this guy a lot easier. The slice looked surgical, meaning a sharp blade. No multiple stab wounds, either. It only took one. He was precise."

"Okay, okay," Tucker groaned. "Can I smoke in here?"

"Don't I wish. You'll get us both busted."

"I seem to be smoking a lot more these days," he mumbled. "I oughta quit."

"And why are you here again?" she asked, clearly ready for him to leave.

"Everyone keeps asking me that. I'm beginning to wonder, too."

She tried to smile, but it didn't quite work. Her upper lip snarled instead. She looked tired, worn out, and lonely. Tucker detected a near kindred spirit, but didn't tell her that.

"They're shipping him back to Oklahoma. That's where you can probably do the most good. Help the family, the arrangements, whatever."

"It's going to sound funny, Detective Phelps, but I needed a purpose," he said. A silence followed. She couldn't make anything out of that, she needed facts, not philosophy.

He tried again: "I needed to find out why."

"That's my job," she corrected, "not yours."

"He was searching for something."

"Like what?"

"The holy grail."

"Get on out of here. I have enough cranks to deal with as it is," she said without raising her voice. "Go on, go."

Tucker told her everything from the Sunday night visit in his car to the videos sent to him and the break-ins. She absorbed it and filed it away. She didn't need to take notes, which Tucker found odd considering Stiles lived by them.

"I've been on the phone with Detective Stiles. We talked earlier today. I know all of this."

Tucker, exasperated himself, held up his hands to get her to stop talking. "Yes, but what I'm telling you, is that it may not be what everyone else thinks of as a 'holy grail.' Value is in the eye of the beholder. We're not talking some rare string of pearls here, or a stack of missing coins. This could be something only a collector would understand."

"I understand collectibles, Mr. Niles."

"He said he found what everyone else had been looking for."

"And what is it then?"

He shook his head.

"So you can't help me?" she asked clearly ready for him to vacate the premises.

"I thought I was by coming down here."

"Sure. You verified everything I already knew, which you could've done over the phone and saved yourself the airplane ticket," she said, nearly growling.

"Feeling helpless isn't something I can put a price tag on," he said. Had he heard that line in some show? If not, he wished he had.

"I see that. Now go, please. I have to get back at it and indigestion is going to hit any minute now and when it does, I'm a bear."

"I appreciate your time."

"Hey, Mr. Niles," she said, stopping him at the door. "The advice is, see our town, hop on a plane, and bury your friend. I'm not interested in you trying to figure this out for me."

"I can see that."

"Good. That's a good thing. Bye now."

Chapter Nine

The get together that night started off well enough with finger sandwiches offered with bowls of chips and salsa. Within an hour, misgivings about the interloper in the midst were whispered from lip to ear. Two hours, along with a concoction mixed in the sink, and a wake erupted with Tucker being everyone's new friend.

"He didn't tell me a thing, the jerk," Rhonda Wilkins said without so much as a slur. She held her liquor well. "I love Bobby, I do," she added. "But he refused to tell us about what he was doing. Not even a hint."

Tucker admired her silky blonde hair over fake-baked shoulders, which reminded him of home, of Courtney. Why did he think of her? And at that moment? Rhonda scooped another drink from the sink.

"Bobby always used to call us his 'collector friends.' He said he kept his buddies compartmentalized. It made it easier to keep up with them that way," she said in between gulps of the purple brew. "I just wanted a shot at buying a couple of transcription discs."

"Which ones?" Tucker asked as a couple of the others guffawed loudly from the kitchen. Apparently one of them—Lee Edwards—funneled something with too much foam in it and nearly choked.

"He said he had a couple of *Mr. and Mrs. North* he wanted to unload." She saw the bewilderment on his face. "I know they're not worth anything. I just like the show and wanted a couple of the ETs." She upended the cup into her mouth.

Jacob Peabody shot into the room with a flourish. A line of purple gracing his upper lip; he appeared impish almost to a fault, but Tucker sensed a sharp mind swimming underneath. He grabbed Rhonda by the waist and planted a kiss on her cheek. She accepted greedily and returned the favor.

"I was hoping for an *Og, Son of Fire*," Jacob said. The house got quiet for a half a second and then uncontrolled laughter followed.

The running gag with OTR fans stemmed from a radio show that existed, but no scripts or recordings have ever been found. The show ran, there's evidence for it, but not from the actual program itself. To the hardcore it gave hope of being the one, but to the realistic it produced laughter. If one episode hadn't surfaced by now, none would.

Tucker filed it away. He knew about *Og*, but it held little interest for him as it told the story of a caveman boy who made pets of prehistoric creatures, learned how to use fire, and hung out with his teenager cave friends. Popular as a series of short stories, the tale took the airwaves, had its run, and disappeared into the sands of time and into legend, which seemed fitting to Tucker being the show that it was.

Would Bobby chase a nonexistent episode in hopes of busting the myth story?

He would mull it over later. For the moment he visited with Bobby's cronies and avoided the punch in the sink.

Jacob caught him by the sleeve and pulled him close. He whispered: "I'm going to tell you right now, Tucker, I didn't like your friend." He said it as a threat, but Tucker knew a bully when he saw one.

"He could be eccentric, I know," he said.

"He also horned in on things around here," he hissed back. Tucker took the reference to be Rhonda. Jacob's lascivious gaze in her direction gave him the answer. "I didn't like that."

"You've got nothing to worry about now," Tucker said none too carefully. He hated bullies, loathed them, in fact. "And I've got news for you, he didn't let anything distract him from what he really wanted."

"That's what you think."

Yet another scrap for Tucker to mull over later.

"I think we should stay up all night long and listen to all seven episodes of Welles' *Les Miserables*!" Tucker turned to see Dave shouting from the top of his countertop near the sink. They laughed at the joke. Surely a master work for Welles, but seven hours is five too many, Tucker thought.

Plastic cups clinked together to honor Bobby. Even Jacob clinked a glass or two, but inebriated as he was, he didn't know who the toast was for. He leaned on Rhonda, who shoved him with what intoxicated strength she had. Jacob's bulky frame pinned her to the counter on several occasions. A couple of times he pressed his pelvis hard against her, which received a resounding head butt. Jacob shook it off with another gulp from his cup.

Lee, the one choking on the funnel earlier, watched everything everyone did with scrutiny as if cataloguing for a nature program. The more intoxicated he became the sharper his glare. Tucker looked away many times to avoid the peering eyes, the probing stares. Without warning, he slung his arm over Tucker's shoulders and pulled him into the living room. Cat calls chased them. Bleary whistles echoed against the walls.

"We're not much help, are we?" Lee asked, suddenly appearing very sober.

"I don't know about that."

"Dead or not, we all want to know what Bobby was after. If not for ourselves, just to know. Knowledge is power in any hobby. And ours most of all. Wouldn't you agree?"

"I would at that."

"You collect?"

"Only what I like to listen to and in no particular format."

"You're a Philistine," Lee said stone-faced.

"I've been called worse."

"To me that's as bad as it gets. Bobby fed his hobby the right way."

"If there is a right way."

"Oh, there is, Tucker. There is absolutely. And it's not mp3s or downloading for free off the internet."

"It's transcription discs all the way, is it?" Tucker asked already knowing the answer.

"To the true collector, you better believe it."

"I just want to know what happened to Bobby."

Lee shrugged his shoulders and then slipped his arm through Tucker's. "Who will get his collection, do you know? Will it go on the market? Will his heirs want to do that, do you think? I'd love first crack. You could put a good word in for me, couldn't you?"

Tucker balled up his fist to rattle a couple of teeth loose, but thought better of it. He didn't dare get into a fist fight. He didn't care for violence and he sure didn't want to antagonize anyone who might be able to tell him about Bobby's last few days on this earth. That's all he really wanted to know.

"I'm not sure. It's really the last thing on my mind," Tucker said.

"Right, sure. How stupid of me. I guess deep down we're all greedy jerks," Lee said not believing a word of it. "If you find out, let me know."

"I'm sure the word will get out."

Lee belched and beat his chest like Tarzan. "Time to fill another funnel!" he proclaimed and disappeared into the kitchen.

Dave eased up beside Tucker with a drink offered in his hand. "It's not really what you expected, huh?"

Tucker took the drink, but only tasted the obligatory sip. "People are people wherever you go, I guess."

"Lee's a jerk most of the time, but really cares for the hobby. Rhonda is warm for anyone's form. And Jacob would like to be that guy, but for some strange reason she's not interested. In everybody else, you better believe it, but not Jacob."

"You?" Tucker asked without thinking.

Dave didn't blink. "Yeah. In the trade we call her 'old faithful,' but not out of spite. We're all too dumb to see she's never going to change and she can't believe the party will ever end."

"And she's into old time radio?"

"Oh man, she's a nut for it. She's got a great collection, which you ought to see and she's read up on everything printed." Dave shrugged as he finished off his drink. "But we all have our idiosyncrasies, don't we? And hers is preying on anything with two legs and a willing libido."

"Except for Jacob's."

"Except for him, that's right."

"And Lee?"

Dave snorted. "We used to pass her back and forth. He'd be after her for a while and then he'd get bored and then it'd be my turn."

"That's pretty twisted."

"Whatever floats your boat, Tucker."

"What about Bobby?"

Dave crushed his plastic cup slowly. He wadded it into a ball and held it in his fist. Either he wanted another cup or the thought of Bobby with Rhonda ate at him. Tucker couldn't tell which.

He shot the cup like a basketball into the kitchen hitting Lee on the side of the face. A few playful words exchanged, but Dave didn't answer the question.

"What about Bobby?" Tucker repeated.

"I don't really know, man. You'll have to ask her. But be careful, in about an hour or so she'll be feeling no pain and will want to drag you off somewhere."

"Great," Tucker groaned.

"Just tellin' ya how she plays it."

"Do you guys party like this all the time?"

"Only when we're together. And pretty soon we're all going to have to play like grown-ups, but some of us don't know it." He clapped his hands for Lee who downed another funnel full of beer. "This'll all catch up with us one day."

"Yeah, it sure will," Tucker agreed, but Dave didn't hear him. He'd already plunged back into the carrying on in the kitchen.

Tucker found a potted plant stuffed into a corner of the living room. He eased over nonchalantly and poured the purple punch into the pot. He hoped it wouldn't kill the wretched plant, but he couldn't afford to get tipsy around this bunch. He didn't really drink anyway, but he made sure that tonight he would keep a clear head.

Jacob plopped down on the floor near him with yet another drink clutched in his fist. Tucker sat down beside him waiting for Jacob to tell him why he didn't like Bobby. It couldn't have been just Rhonda, but you never knew. He leaned against the wall near a floor lamp and waited.

He didn't wait long. "Bobby would be in a back room about now searching for something on the internet. And it wouldn't be five minutes and Rhonda would go traipsing right after him. He drove us all crazy when he came out bragging about some other show he'd tracked down through some contact."

"Who?"

"What's that?"

"Contact? Who are you talking about?"

"Oh, anybody. He had connections in the trade all over the country. And none of them gets it. There isn't any money to be made in this hobby. I've tried."

"You've run a booth at a convention?"

"Which one haven't I run a booth at?" Jacob said stumbling through a few syllables. "I've been to Mid-Atlantic, the one in Cincinnati, Seattle, and the Friends of Old Time Radio."

"In New Jersey?"

"That's the one. I barely made enough to pay all my expenses. A round trip ticket, hotel, booth rental, and food adds up after a while. No one in this lousy hobby gets it."

"Unless it's a missing show like *Og*."

Jacob fired a gun with his fingers. "Bull's eye, buddy boy. Lots of dealers love to brag and talk shop and talk big about what all they know, but it's all the same. Nobody's making a dime out of it."

"Then why do it?"

Jacob got an intoxicated grin on his face. "Remember the first time you heard a show, a really good show, and it transported you. You did all the work. All they had was sound effects and voices. That's it. You did all the rest."

"I remember."

"That's why. That is something that Bobby and I did have in common. He was passionate about it."

"Yes, he was."

"And a little crazy," Jacob said.

"That, too."

From across the room, Rhonda blew kisses their way. Jacob played along grabbing a couple out of the air. She winked, but not at Jacob.

"She wants you, man," Jacob said not hiding his contempt.

"I don't want her."

"You're the first then."

"I was married."

For a second Jacob sobered up. "Was?"

"Yeah, she's gone now."

"You loved her?"

"I sure did."

"Love is a crazy thing that makes you do stupid things." He chugged from his cup as much as his mouth would hold.

"Does she know?" Tucker asked.

"About what?"

"How you feel."

Jacob drained the drink in one smooth motion. He banged the back of his head against the wall letting it rest there. "I've tried everything in the book."

"Have you tried telling her?"

Jacob shut his eyes and looked like he fell asleep. Tucker took the cup from his fingers and set on an end table by the flowery couch.

"He pass out?" Rhonda asked as she sauntered over. She ran her fingers through Tucker's hair almost absent-mindedly like she'd done it a thousand times.

"Maybe, not sure." He pulled himself up and away from her probing fingers.

Tucker ventured to say: "He cares about you."

"He shouldn't," was all she could say. "I'm no good. And deep down, he is. We'd make a lousy pair."

"What about you and Bobby?"

"What about me and Bobby?"

"Just that."

She yawned, stretched, and waved goodbye to Lee and Dave. "We'll back be in a few."

They wolf whistled in unison.

"We're going to take a walk," she said, chiding them.

More wolf whistles followed.

"C'mon, let's go for a walk. It's nice out tonight."

The fresh air hit like a tonic to Tucker. The thick party air in Dave's stifled. Night time meant something to him. It meant a lot to his wife. When he had a day off from the station, he would sometimes sit all night on their back porch in the swing they put together one hot afternoon. That night, they cuddled on their new purchase while star gazing. It became a weekend ritual which ended when...

"There's a halo around the moon," Rhonda said, breaking into his thoughts. "That's supposed to mean rain, isn't it?"

"In Oklahoma that's what it means. I'm not sure about up here in Nebraska."

"It does." She laughed at his joke as she threaded her arm through his.

"Nebraska of all places. How in the world Bobby hooked up with all of you is beyond me."

"It's called the internet. He found our group's website and sent an e-mail. As secretary for the group, I answered and sent him an invite to come see us any time he wanted."

"Lincoln, Nebraska isn't known as a hotbed for old time radio trading," Tucker said.

"It's just where there's an appreciation group. There's one in DC and one in Colorado. There's a few at some college campuses here and there. We get together on a semi-regular basis, talk about old shows, listen to a few, and have some laughs."

"And drink."

"We do a lot of that, too. It's just something that brings misfits together to not feel so alone out there in the big, bad, uncaring world," she said. He couldn't tell if the drink talked, or if Rhonda really meant it.

"We all need something."

"We sure do."

"And what about Jacob?" he asked pulling for the guy one more time.

"I'm sure the boys told you all about me and that I would get my claws into you before the night is through."

"Well, will you?" he asked. It wasn't a challenge, but a sad observation about the way she lived her life.

"The night is still young," she shot back without thinking. She didn't mean it and Tucker knew it. They both relaxed as they strolled down the dimly lit streets.

"So," she said, breaking the silence, "are you here like some amateur sleuth to see which one of us did it?"

"Are you telling me one of you did?" he asked, the thought shocked him. It occurred to him, but still shocked.

"I'm not telling you anything of the kind. I'm playing to keep the conversation going."

"Play what if with me then."

"What if one of us killed Bobby?" she asked, not playing anymore.

"Who would it be?"

She took her arm out of his and folded it across her chest. "That's a pretty sick thought. My first question would be why?"

"The obvious."

"Over a radio show?" She laughed harshly. "You have got to be kidding me. We're enthusiasts who can't grow up."

"Collectors do crazy things. Believe me, I know, I was Bobby's friend."

"So was I and I'm telling you none of the guys would even know how to kill someone."

"Taking a life is easy, Rhonda," Tucker told her.

"Not over something like this."

"You heard Jacob. What if it was something like *Og, Son of Fire*. People in the trade would pay a pretty penny to be the first to have it and they in turn would try and flog it."

"What's it really worth, Tucker? I mean, really, come on. It's supposed to be a show about a cave boy who shows his friends how to use fire and domesticates a couple of saber-toothed tigers. It's not top-notch quality, or at least we can speculate that it isn't," she said.

"The quality isn't the issue. It being possibly non-existent is the issue. One of those would put a collector, or enthusiast, at the top of the heap."

"Name one who thinks like that."

"Bobby did."

"Besides Bobby."

"You? The guys you run around with?"

"You've seen us," she said, now agitated with him. "Jacob can't get over his feelings for me, Lee is a self-centered idiot who can barely tie his own shoe laces, and Dave…well, he's just Dave."

"What's his deal, anyway? Nobody talks much about Dave."

"That's by design," she said as she pointed up at a star in the sky. "I love looking at the stars. Always have. Dave's a lot like that star. He's bright and sparkles a lot, but is far away."

"Doesn't mean he didn't kill Bobby," Tucker threw at her.

"You should know that a collector, a real, hardcore collector, collects so he's the only one who has something, or one of few who has something. It makes him look like a big shot. An enthusiast loves the hobby and collects out of passion for the medium."

"Well put. So a collector killed Bobby?"

"I don't know who killed him and I'm getting tired of talking about it." Tears came to her eyes. She wiped them away frantically willing them to dry up before they could fall. "Now look what you made me do."

Tucker stopped walking. He dug for a handkerchief in his pocket. She wiped away every last trace of a tear with it. She gave it back to him with little ceremony or with thanks.

"I think I get it now," he said. He stuffed the hanky back in his pocket. "I don't know why Bobby didn't tell me."

"Tell you what?"

"About you two."

Another wave of tears welled up in her eyes. She fought hard, but they fell. This time she let them. So did Tucker. He didn't retrieve the hanky because he knew she needed to do it. Grief racked her body. Sobs bubbled on her lips while her body shook all over. They stood there for five minutes while she cried.

"So as Jacob is to you, you were to Bobby," he said as the wailing died down. "Is that how it was?"

She shook her head.

"I thought as much. Did Bobby ever know how you felt?"

Another shake of her head was her answer.

"And so you burn up through as many guys as possible as some weird way of coping," he added as an afterthought.

"That sounds about right," she said quietly.

"I want to give you some kind of comfort and tell you he cared about you, too, Rhonda, but he never mentioned you to me. Or, any of you, for that matter. He kept us all compartmentalized, I think. That was his way of handling the world. I was his radio buddy back home and you were his contacts out in the world."

"You're saying he used me…us?" she asked with the threat of more tears following.

"Not at all. I think he lived in a make believe world where the flowers always grew, the good guys always won, and he lived as king. He was the hero in his own little fairyland barely touching reality and avoided it whenever possible."

"That's probably true. He could talk for hours about some show or other and tell you everything there was to know about it. It drove a lot of the dealers crazy at the conventions."

"Anyone crazed enough to kill him?"

"In a trivia contest, maybe, but not with a knife. Not like that. Let's go back."

She put her arm through his again. This time she held him tighter, closer to her. Not because she wanted him, but because she craved the comfort she couldn't get from any of her string of men.

"You need to come see my collection," she invited.

"I'd like that. Tomorrow?"

"Sure. I'm off tomorrow. Come over at lunchtime and I'll have us some burgers, or something. Sound good?"

"The best invitation I've had since getting here."

They fell into a conversation about their favorite radio shows, the ones they liked, the ones they loathed, and the ones they admired, but didn't necessarily count among their top ten. He found her easy to talk to and made note of the phrases that sounded like something Bobby would say. She used the term "holy grail" a couple of times, which caught his attention, but didn't have any meaning beyond just looking for the hard to find. It's too bad Bobby wasn't attracted to her, Tucker thought. He could have used a woman like this in his life on a permanent basis. Underneath the partying and string of men, Rhonda seemed to ache for someone to keep her rooted, anchored. Too bad Bobby didn't see that.

"Could you take me to any of his haunts while I'm here?" he asked out of the blue.

"You mean dealers or collectors?"

"That's what I mean. I'm not sure they know any better than the rest of us what he was after."

"Why didn't he tell anyone?" he asked out loud.

"Because it really was the holy grail, I think. I'd seen him hot after stuff before, but not like this. He said he had to be careful."

"Why is that?" he asked before realizing how stupid the question was. Because someone wanted him dead.

She didn't answer. "He did say that every hobby, field of study, or religion has its own holy grail. Its own sacred thing that everyone wants or lusts after."

"And he'd found it."

"I think he did."

Chapter Ten

Tucker fell out of bed before six, which irked him as he didn't have a job to go to that morning. He tumbled to the floor, stretched, thought about going back to bed, thought better of it and dug in his suitcase for a pair of clean boxers. His teeth had grown fur and he felt dingy. He hadn't showered since Oklahoma.

Whoever rifled through his unmentionables didn't do a very good job of hiding it as his clothes were all mixed together. He wondered if the same person who searched his luggage was the same one who woke him up early in the morning by shutting his door none too quietly.

After his shower, Tucker found the coffee pot with a note from Dave taped to it. Instructions for breakfast were actually directions to a "killer" donut shop within walking distance. Dave, already work-ward bound, left a half pot for him.

Pouring his first cup of the day, Tucker gaped at the horrible mess left from last night's party royal. Empty pizza boxes, cups, bottles, beer cans, a dirty funnel seemed to erupt from the kitchen floor. In the sink a purple muck lined the drain. He hadn't seen carnage like this since his frat days in college. Little wonder he gave up the frat life.

He devoured a couple of fresh éclairs from the donut shop dubbed "Hot Dough," which he found to be a horrible name for anything. The éclairs made up for it, though, as they melted in his mouth. More coffee in a cup-to-go and he took off down the busiest street next to the donut shop.

Staring at nothing in particular, he drifted back to last night's festivities. One loved Bobby, one jealous of him, another indifferent, and yet one more greedy for his collection. Isn't that the way with people, he thought. No one on the planet got the same reaction from any half dozen of their friends or acquaintances. We're all lover, warrior, king, loser, liar, and thief, he thought wearily as he plodded along the sidewalk. He hoped the day would fly so he could hop a plane and go back home. He didn't want to be there anymore.

A horn beeped at him from behind.

"You're up and at 'em bright and early," Rhonda said, looking none too worse for wear considering her drinking and emotional outburst from just a few hours ago. "I was on my way to Dave's when I saw you walking. You look lost."

"I am lost. I don't know this town."

"Come on, I'll show you around while we wait for a couple of the stores to open up."

They drove aimlessly through the congested streets in Lincoln. They explored downtown with Rhonda pointing out a landmark or hot spot. She passed by the university, which Tucker blew a raspberry to in mock disgust. She frowned at him.

"Sorry, I'm from Oklahoma and a Sooner fan. We don't like the Cornhuskers," he said.

"So I've heard."

"Beautiful campus, though."

"I graduated from there. Good school."

"In?"

"What else? English."

He laughed at that. "Oh no, an English major! Let me guess, you loved the classics."

"Only if there is a steampunk version of them. And that's stretching it. I liked the poetry and the grammar, heaven help me. My thing was creative writing."

"A creative writing...uh, person?" he asked with a mock smile.

"I wanted to teach it, if you can believe that." She turned a corner pointing out a pizza joint. "I wrote many a love poem there."

"Another Shelley or Lord Byron?" he asked.

"Neither. In my poems the guy always dies for some awful reason. Don't ask me."

He swirled the last swig of coffee and downed it.

"Need a refill?" she asked.

"No way. I'll need to recycle some coffee pretty soon as it is."

"We'll go to Randy's first then. He has a restroom."

Turning on her blinker, Rhonda whipped into the left lane and then turned into a narrow street with a few shops on it. A red-striped awning decorated a bakery bragging about "gluten-free" muffins, a pink door offered the services of a seamstress, and a cruddy faded gray paint job graced the front of a place called "Trader Book's."

"Clever," Tucker commented.

"You don't know the half of it. The guy's a kook, but knows a little bit about everything, Sherlock Holmes, especially the radio run, military supplies and regalia, history, and comic books. A few years back he ran an Army surplus store."

"Ah, one of those types."

She parked, swiped the parking toll in the meter, and barged into Trader Book's. Tucker tagged along behind her. The glare from the morning sun couldn't compare to the dark shadows awaiting them in the book store. Cramped shelves littered the floor in no obvious order or organization. A cat rested languidly on a desk shoved into a corner piled neck deep in hard back books. In the back the sound of a saw buzzed angrily.

"Randy!" Rhonda shouted above the saw. "Hey, hey!"

The saw shut off and a short, tubby man entered the room. He reminded Tucker of a dwarf from a fairy tale. The man ceremoniously kissed Rhonda's hand to which she submitted willingly. He bowed. She curtsied.

"Randy Shaw," he said holding out stubby, but strong fingers to Tucker. "You're the DJ from Oklahoma. What station?"

"KLMA."

"The Llama?" the little man asked.

"Yes. How'd you know? We're a mid-sized independent nearly out in the sticks."

"Bobby told me about you and where you worked. I found your website and listen in from time to time. I like your Led Zepplin hour on Saturdays."

"You and half the county back home."

"The chase then," Randy said. He waddled to a book shelf and squinted to see the titles.

"Excuse me?"

"As in cut to the…chase." He didn't take his eyes off the spines of the books. "They're not worth what they should be worth, you know. The older they are, for sure, but anything within the past thirty years or so is hardly worth much. I should know, I have stacks of them in the back collecting dust mites like Rhonda there collects notches on her belt."

"Randy!"

"Sorry, dear, only joking."

"I know, but still," she said with mock indignation. He bowed. She curtsied. Tucker wondered if this would go on all morning.

"What are you talking about, Mr. Shaw?" Tucker asked.

"It's Trader Book, or Randy, but not Mr. Shaw."

"Trader Book?"

"As in Trader Vic's."

"I got that," Tucker said. He waited for an answer.

"I don't know really," Randy said. "Maybe I dreamed it. I don't know. It sounds medieval, which is my period of interest. I love all that torture and Spanish Inquisition. Don't you? If not, you should become a fan and I don't mean of the Monty Python sketch, either." He said it all in one breath.

"What are you looking for?"

"Your quest brought you here and I assume it is about dear Bobby, so I bring the answer to all your questions." He jerked a volume off the shelf and nearly slammed it melodramatically on an empty table. The only one in the establishment, Tucker noticed.

"Comic books?" he asked looking at the Comic Book Price Guide. "You're kidding me, aren't you?"

Randy looked perplexed, turned to Rhonda, and held open his arms. She shook her head no.

"Bobby collected and gave me first crack at some of the twelve-centers he owned. They're really the last frontier for collectors right now."

"I'm not here about comic books."

"Hey, don't mock, buddy, I sold a *Batman* number eight that netted me forty grand not too long ago," he bragged. Tucker had seen arrogance before, but this guy patented a brand all his own.

"That's great, but I'm not interested in comics."

"Bobby always was. That's how we met. He sold me a Ringo Kidd with the gloss still shimmering on the cover." He dug in his pocket for nose spray, shook it up, and shot a squirt into his nostrils. "Hay fever," he explained.

"Old time radio shows. ETs, that sort of thing," Tucker said. "Bobby's interest in comics was to pass the time when he wasn't chasing down a transcription disc somewhere."

"Oh, my friend Tucker, we are at cross purposes here. I say comic books, you say radio shows, which is it to be?"

"Quit yanking his chain, Randy," Rhonda chided from a corner of the shop. Tucker noticed her thumbing through a stack of thin volumes, presumably poetry. "He's only here 'til tomorrow. He doesn't have all day."

Randy snorted another round of nose spray. He pinched his nostrils together. He voice sounded muffled. "But he was my go-to guy for comic books, Rhonda. He could track a Detective Comics like a bloodhound."

"Radio shows, Randy," she said.

"Bobby was nuts about them," he said as he closed the cover on the comic price guide. "And I don't mean nuts as in crazy about, but I mean nuts as in obsessed, as in certifiable. That's what I'm talking about."

"That's what I want to know about," Tucker said. "I don't know if it has anything to do with the way he died, but I want to know what he was chasing."

"So does everybody who knew him." He placed the book back on the shelf. "A cup of joe?"

"No, thank you."

"Rhonda?"

"Yeah, sure. Cream and sugar."

"But of course. One never forgets how a lady takes her java." He lumbered to a pot near the cash register and prepared a couple of mugs with a Trader Book's logo stamped on both of them.

"He was onto something that he thought was big," Tucker said, getting the conversation back on track.

"I remember when he found an Abe Burrows that no one else knew about. He nearly danced out of his clothes and into the street. And to think that show was sponsored by Listerine toothpaste. Yuck-o-la!" He handed a mug to Rhonda, who blew the steam away.

"Yeah, he did the same thing when he found an episode of *Zorro* hidden away at a radio station in Idaho," Tucker added. "He loved it."

"As I said, dear man, he was a loon. Friend, or not, you've got to admit he could come unhinged when he found a stray transcription disc."

"He would sometimes run his fingernail in the grooves to see if the voices would vibrate enough to hear them."

"You see? Certifiable. Not that I didn't like the guy. I did. But, come on, really? It's an old radio show. Who even knows about them anymore? Only a few rabid fans and even fruitier collectors who overstate the value of the hobby they happen to be in and love so much."

"What about you and comic books?" Rhonda asked casually, joining the conversation.

"That's different, m'lady, and you know it. Where's a pricing guide for old radio shows? There isn't one. You have to depend on the knowledge of the idiot collector, who inflates his importance and the significance of the show to some doe-eyed stranger who doesn't know the difference between *The Adventures of Ellery Queen* and *One Man's Family.*"

"Did he come and see you?" Tucker asked.

"Why would he?" was the response.

"You're a very careful person, aren't you, Randy? You haven't answered much of anything since we got here."

"I didn't realize this was the inquisition."

"I thought you liked the inquisition?"

"*Touché.* Aren't you the clever fellow? Yes, he saw me on Tuesday and before you ask, I already told this to the police."

"Detective Phelps?"

"A lovely lass, if it weren't for the road map eyes of hers," Randy said offhandedly. "She picked the wrong profession."

"What did he want, Randy?" Rhonda asked.

"Believe it or not, he was curious about oil."

Rhonda grabbed a book and shook it at Randy. "This isn't the time for your jokes. The man is asking a civil question and you're giving him grief. Bobby was murdered, Randy, or need I remind you?"

Randy snatched the book out of her hand. "I am serious as a heart attack. He wanted to know if we could track down information on an oil company."

"Which one?"

"A-1 Oil and Gas. They're out of, or were, out of Louisiana."

"Were?" Tucker asked.

"They're defunct now and that's about all I know."

"Randy," Rhonda warned.

"On a stack of comic books, fair one," he swore.

"That's good enough for me. Let's go, Tucker. I need a decent cup of coffee."

The ride to Rhonda's apartment unsettled Tucker. The maze of Midwestern streets with their clean, clipped lawns, aged trees, and uniform cookie cutter houses didn't appeal this early in the morning. His solace he found deep in the recesses of a fertile imagination where he conquered or vanquished as some archetypal Jungian hero. He silently cursed the Psychology 101 class he took in college for sending him down this road, but it clarified a monstrous and uncaring world.

Like Br'er Rabbit, he jumped head first into his happy place, which consisted of him sitting in his living room chair melting into the sounds of a favorite show reverberating from his ancient stereo system. The simplicity of the morals, the standard of ethics, the code of living that permeated from the airwaves grounded him, gave him comfort. Others disappeared willingly into the covers of a book, and still some erased their minds with countless hours of movies, TV, and the internet. He bottled himself in the imagination of the past. That, he understood. That gave meaning.

The still voice in his brain was telling him the trip, though valiant an effort, was a waste. He couldn't conduct any kind of investigation. He wasn't a detective. In his fantasy life, sure, but in the end a fantasy only existed on the movie screen of his mind. Bobby had been murdered not as a chance meeting in a quiet hotel hallway, but by wicked design. To think it rooted in a stupid collectible boggled.

But there could be no other reason.

"We're here," Rhonda said snapping him out of his trance. He longed to be home and it showed on his face. "This isn't really what you expected, was it?" she asked. "Your trip, I mean."

"To tell the truth, I don't know what I expected. All of Bobby's contacts…there could be dozens, hundreds of them. And this is just Lincoln, Nebraska. What about in Cincinnati and the convention folks? This could go on forever."

She parked in from of a building labeled F in bright neon green, which Tucker found distasteful. She locked up the car and led the way through a honeycomb of apartments.

"Second floor," she directed.

A soda and peanut butter sandwich later, Tucker found himself thumbing through a box of mp3 discs of

Rhonda's radio show collection. She pointed out her "faves," as she called them, with passionate determination that she deserved to be in the hobby. Tucker heard it before from others who just liked listening to the shows. They didn't have to know every title of every show with every date and time stamped in their memory banks like some fans did. People who knew more than others always set themselves apart from the rest of the herd, which Tucker gave up after the car crash.

He thought of Bobby. His friend's mind worked like an online encyclopedia tuned into the frequency of the past, specifically the late 1920s to the early 60s when radio played a very different tune.

"We would sit here and listen for hours just talking. You know, discussing what we knew about this radio actor, or writer, or famous director," Rhonda explained. "I wanted to be so close to him so I read up on everything I could find."

"Dunning's book?"

"Yeah, and Cox and Grams, who I met once and found very charming."

"They both know a lot about the shows and who put them together. They have some good books out there," he agreed.

"I found Randy disturbing," he said suddenly changing the subject.

"You have to get to know Trader Book to understand him. He's a lot of smoke and mirrors because that's the only way people find him interesting. He was picked on as a kid and teenager, which he hated, so that's his way of feeling important."

"You're defending him?"

"I understand him."

"Bobby was bullied, too."

"Yeah, he talked about it from time to time. It was really the only chance I got to know what he was all about," she said.

"There's too much grieving in this room," Tucker said. He got up and found her bathroom. He recycled the morning coffee, washed up, and passed by the second bedroom of the apartment.

He stopped to give it the once over. Had he seen this room before somewhere? Surely not. How could he..? He snapped his fingers.

"Rhonda," he beckoned.

"Yeah." She joined him in the hallway with a questioning look on her face. "What's up?"

"The jig is."

"What are you talking about?"

"Where's your computer?" he asked knowing full well where it was. He moved a couple of chairs out of way near a desk by the bed.

"Tucker, what's eating you?"

"Let me login into my e-mail account and I'll show you."

"Feel free."

"I will." He logged in, typed in his password, and opened up his inbox. A list of e-mails work related, a couple from family members, and one from Stiles filled the screen. He scrolled down and found the one he wanted. He tapped the mouse a couple of times.

The second video of Bobby popped to life. He enticed Tucker to make the trip to Lincoln because of a promised find that he wanted show everyone on the weekend. Tucker let it play to the end.

"Look familiar?" he asked.

"Yes," she answered still staring at the screen. "He sent it from here."

"I would say from the set dressing that was obvious."

"What are you so angry about all of the sudden? I'm not denying anything," she countered. "So he shot the video here."

"You were in the room. There's a shadow over on the far left of a person," he accused.

"So what if I was in the room?"

"You heard what he said. I'd forgotten about it until I watched it again just now."

"What's that?"

"He wanted to show everyone what he'd tracked down, Rhonda. It wasn't just a pipe dream at that moment. That didn't click until now. Whatever it was, he found it. You heard him, you were here. He wanted to show everybody this weekend."

"So what are you saying then?" she asked nearly frantic.

"You were in the room with him. You were hanging out with him while he was here."

He leaned closer to her and she jumped to her feet.

"You're saying that I know what this is all about?"

"You better believe it."

"And what? I've been stringing you along this whole time? Is that it?" Her voice raised an octave.

"I've known folks to get their jollies off for a whole lot less," he said, suddenly filled with confidence that he didn't know he had.

"You heard the message, Tucker. He was enigmatic and weird, just like always. He wasn't about to tell me. Sure, I've already admitted how I felt about him, but he didn't feel the same. I would have done anything for him and you know it!"

"That's exactly right, Rhonda. You would."

"But not cover up what may have gotten him killed." Instead of continuing to raise her volume, she became quiet, still. "Never in a million years would you do that."

"But he wanted to show us."

"Yes."

"You were here with him."

"He said he would let everyone in on it come the weekend. With him getting killed I'd let it slip my mind."

"Not likely."

"Okay, I see why you're jumping to the conclusion you're making, Tucker. You let it slip your mind, too."

"That's true," he conceded. "I did."

"He wouldn't tell me. He wouldn't tell any of us."

"But he had it when he made the video and sent it," he said trying to fill in the gaps. "Or, knew where 'it' was."

"I'm suddenly getting very scared."

"What for?"

"It had to be what got him killed, Tucker. Had to be. And whatever it was, no matter what it was, means so much to someone that they are willing to take a life to keep it or protect it." A lone tear slid down her face.

"No hanky this time," he told her. She laughed, which produced more tears. "And with you, I'm scared."

"Maybe we should just stop then."

"Not a chance."

"We don't have anything else."

"Oh yes, we do."

"What?"

"The A-1 oil company." He cracked his knuckled with a flourish. "It's time to let the fingers do the digging."

The rest of the afternoon Tucker surfed the 'net searching for every single scrap of info tagged for an "A-1 Oil and Gas company" out of Louisiana. He soon discovered that scrap may be all he would get. Rhonda sat beside him eagerly assisting in any way possible. She called any phone number he found and made notes along the way.

A few credit card purchases later to online newspaper archives, and Tucker waded through a handful of articles dated from the 1940s and 50s about an A-1 Standard Gas and Oil Company located in Alexandria, Louisiana. The owner, Robert Bellevue, a wildcatter from the 1920s settled down in '40 to build his own company. An article or two hinted at eccentricities without giving details. The trail dried up pretty quick after that.

"I can't find a thing about it after 1960," Tucker said pushing away from the computer. "I can't make heads or tails as to why this even means a thing, and much less why it would matter to Bobby. I feel like Sam Spade on the radio where there's that bit of information scratching at the back of my mind, but I can't get at it. It's frustrating."

"Was he a collector, do you think?" Rhonda asked believing she'd stumbled on something revealing.

"If that's what 'eccentricities' means, I guess. I don't know."

"Who would?"

"Would any of the guys?" he asked. "Jacob? Dave?"

She frowned at the idea. "Hmm…maybe…" She pulled her chair in front of the computer and pecked at the keyboard.

"What does that mean?" Tucker asked with a wry grin on his face.

"It means 'hmm.' I got to thinking about a girl that Bobby used to date online."

Tucker's jaw fell a mile. "Say what?"

"Yeah, I know. Here I was in the flesh all over him half the time, but he felt safer kissing on cyberspace. Go fig."

"What's her name?"

"Andie something. Clurman, I think. She might have a notion about what he was after."

"Does she know about..?" He let the question hang in the air.

"She does. Lee told her on the phone. She went all hysterical." She held up her empty glass. "Would you mind?"

"Oh, I get it. I need to leave the room."

"It's not like that. You can meet her. It's just I can't track her down and talk to you at the same time."

Tucker found some Kool-Aid packets, chose the Black Cherry, and found the sugar and a pitcher. Stirring the batch as he walked back into the bedroom he heard Rhonda and another, very feminine voice, conversing.

"I'm just asking, Andie; I don't have any ulterior motive here," Rhonda pleaded.

"Bobby and I had a pretty serious thing, Rhonda. I thought you understood that," the girl named Andie whined from the computer screen.

Tucker sat down beside Rhonda and introduced himself, explained everything since the night of Bobby's mysterious visit to KLMA, and waited.

"I don't know much," Andie said. Tucker saw her look down at her keyboard and type something.

"The value you have in this, Andie," Tucker said carefully, "is that we have an inkling as to what Bobby was after."

"I really do not know. After our thing we didn't talk much."

"But you talked," Rhonda reminded her. "Bobby said you did. Not all the time, but some."

"We know he was asking around about an old oil company in Louisiana. It was called A-1," Tucker said. "That ring a bell?"

Andie's eyes bugged out in instant recognition. She typed furiously at her keyboard.

"Andie?" Rhonda said.

"Hold on, hold on."

She scanned something on her screen mumbling along as she read it. Another few taps on her computer and grinned in triumph.

"Robert Bellevue."

"I think I said that already," Tucker said. He tasted the Kool-Aid with approval. "He was the owner."

"Yes and a big time collector. He sold out in '61 and built a big house that is now abandoned. He did all kinds of civic projects for his home town and helped build a hospital..." She droned on about other achievements that didn't interest Tucker.

"Wait, wait a minute," he said. "What was it that he had that Bobby wanted to know about? G.I. Joes or baseball cards?"

"Ha! This guy was the mac daddy of old time radio collecting."

"What's that mean?" Rhonda asked.

"Ninety thousand shows, at least, is what I mean," Andie bragged.

"With mp3s that wouldn't take much," Rhonda retorted, trying hard to burst Andie's bubble. Tucker detected the jealousy, but didn't understand it. How could a cyberspace relationship compare to the real thing?

"In the late sixties and seventies? Bellevue collected the ETs, girl."

"Now we're getting somewhere," Tucker said. "Thank you, Andie."

Chapter Eleven

His final night there, Tucker and company went out to eat Italian at a dive called "Georgio's" close to the university. College students of every shape and size ate, drank, and made arrangements for late night parties at friend's houses. Tucker could barely hear anything at their table shoved snugly near the front window of the restaurant.

He made Rhonda promise to keep a zipped lip about what they'd found out about Bellevue and Bobby's interest in him. They tried to pick up more scraps, but came up empty of anything interesting. The rumor mill online reported that Bellevue had died back in '89 leaving his entire estate to a lonely widow. The mill also enticed collectors into thinking he squirreled away a treasure trove of recordings that he alone listened to in the comfort of his mansion. Supposedly the widow still lived in hopes of cashing in on her late husband's horde.

Lee got a call on his cell, looked at the number, and nearly went white. He held up a finger to the others and disappeared out on the sidewalk to take the call.

"You never know with Lee," Jacob remarked through a mouthful of linguini. "That guy has so many irons in the fire."

"I thought of someone else that Bobby may have talked to," Dave said. He raised a hand to the waitress for a refill on his Pepsi. "Julia Appleton."

"Who's that?" Tucker asked.

"A professor."

"Who did Bobby *not* talk to? Maybe that's a better question," Rhonda said. She finished her Alfredo earlier and sipped at a cappuccino.

"I don't know if he talked to her or not, but she knows a lot about the audio history."

"Where does she teach?"

"KU in Lawrence," Dave said. "A Jayhawk."

"Bobby really did keep every contact close to the vest, didn't he?" Tucker asked no one in particular. "What's her name?"

"Julia Appleton. I've talked to her a few times as well. She's great."

"What have I missed?" Randy Stark boomed three tables away.

"Who invited him?" Jacob asked not containing his distaste for the man.

Randy pulled up a chair, refused a menu, ordered a pitcher of beer with one cup and joined into the conversation with reckless abandon.

"Find what you were looking for, Tucker?" he asked finally.

"If you mean more questions, then sure. Not much else. I'm ready to go home and get ready for the funeral and let it lie."

"Back to..? Where was it again?" Jacob asked.

"Lyle, Oklahoma."

Lee slumped in his seat. He barely acknowledged Randy with a quick nod. The mood shifted. His ever-eager smile now replaced with a deep frown, Lee kept his part of the conversation clipped and to the point. He also looked at his phone from time to time with trepidation.

Tucker took all of this in, but didn't push for an explanation. He said the truth. He was ready to go home. He needed his job, his quiet time in the evenings, and a return to some kind of normalcy. He couldn't fathom Bobby's quest, but knew for certain it killed him. No matter how absurd or surreal, he knew that Bobby dug in the wrong place and paid for it with his life.

He and Rhonda did a little digging that afternoon. Would it bring either of them harm as well? The thought sobered him. He tried to engage in the conversation, but found it tedious, boring. He could tell that they guarded their words around him, the interloper, the friend of a friend.   Even Rhonda, so talkative earlier, let the others talk without joining in. Her thoughts carried her a thousand miles away where Tucker imagined she and Bobby lived in eternal bliss.

He couldn't, and wouldn't, begrudge her that. He lived with lost bliss every day of his life. Why condemn someone else of the same thing?   Granted, she and Bobby never fully connected, but she needed something of him to keep herself going.

As the group broke up for the night, Rhonda pulled him aside. She stuffed money into his hand.

"What's this for?" Tucker asked her unsure of what she gave him.

"He wouldn't appreciate it, but I can't fly down there for his funeral, and I wanted him to have something from me. Buy some flowers for me, would you?" It sounded like a plea.

"Flowers?"

"I know, I know. He'd hate it, but I wanted to give him something other than what he already had. Does that make sense?"

"Sure. I get it."

"You're a good friend, Tucker," she added. "I hope we'll see you around up here."

"No more questions?"

"About what he was after? I have lots, but what am I going to do about it?"

Somehow he didn't believe her, but let it pass.

"You'll call me or send me an e-mail," she said. "You have my info?"

"Yes, all in my phone."

"Rhonda, I just thought..?" He couldn't finish the sentence. The words dried to dust in his mouth.

"Bobby meant a lot to me, but it wasn't reciprocated. Whatever he was after was another one of his 'things.' A girl moves on. She has to."

"What about Jacob?"

She tried to fake a smile, but failed miserably. "He asked me out again tonight. That has to be the hundredth time."

"And you told him no again."

"No, I actually said yes. The others will make fun and say he's the only one I haven't gone out with."

"What made you change your mind?"

"I don't know. I just did."

"Let me know how that works out."

"I will."

He hopped in Dave's Escape and waved to the rest of them. A sudden grimness overcame him as he pondered that he probably wouldn't see any of them again. Jacob kept his eyes on Rhonda as she found her car in the parking lot. Randy pontificated about some unknown fact about Captain America to Lee who didn't listen as he took another phone call. His gaze never left Tucker as he talked on the phone and waved goodbye.

Chapter Twelve

Bright sunshine filled the bedroom where he slept. Fighting the urge to get on the computer and check his e-mail for hours of mindless catching up with faraway friends, he covered up in their bed. He slept dream-free until supper time.

The flight didn't take long back to OKC, but another hour or so on the road left him fatigued from the whole trip. He couldn't escape the feeling of wasted time. Sure, it was good for him to go, but it didn't fill the void and it sure didn't change anything.

He did it because he needed to prove that he could be there for someone other than himself. That he could be unselfish and brave, with a sense of honor that everyone saw in him. He did it to show that he could actually care.

The last thought he had before falling asleep was that he didn't for his wife. With one final act of selfishness, he set in motion her lone trip along a wet highway to see her parents. In-laws he didn't care for, Tucker found extra commercials to cut at the station to keep him away. She didn't say a cross word about it, sweetly said she loved him, and died in a single car crash an hour later.

Rushing out there as quick as he could in the rain, Tucker punished himself with repeated blows to his leg and a few slaps to the face. Rage became remorse, which changed into fear and loathing, and finally became grief. He wailed in his car on the way. He yelled curses at God. He did every useless thing he could think of before he got to the crash site.

Her body already wrapped inside an ambulance, he ran to the doors of the vehicle and jerked on them in vain. Not much else could he recall after that. He remembered seeing her in the ambulance before viewing her body several times at the funeral home, but couldn't conjure images of it.

All this he thought of before passing out under the covers. Each time he did, it brought on terrible dreams of the wreck from every possible angle and variety of scenario. But this time he didn't dream, or couldn't remember any if he did, which he counted as a blessing.

As he came out of his slumber, he jerked upright. He had a sudden urge to check the house. He hadn't when he got home and with the near break-in before he left for Lincoln, he should have looked the house over. Stiles said he'd have a patrol cruiser check out the neighborhood while he was away, but you never knew.

He scanned room to room, searching for anything out of place. Carefully he checked to see if his wife's sewing room had been disturbed. Since her death, he hadn't touched any item in the room, choosing to let part of her still live in the home they shared for such a short time. The bathrooms were clear, as well as the kitchen, and even the utility room looked the same as he left it.

Clicking the light on in his study, he examined every book on the shelf, every CD and mp3 he owned, his computer desk, and the small oak stand where he stored his miniscule transcription disc collection. A quick count and he breathed a sigh of relief. He chided himself for his paranoia when something caught his attention out of the corner of his eye.

Being methodical, and somewhat anal, Tucker filed everything in order. Books in alphabetical order according to the author's last name, CDs the same way, but the transcription discs were in order based on year. Many of the paper sleeves protecting the discs had seen better days with most stained or discolored from age. Once upon a time, Tucker found a package of sleeves for sale at a flea market. They looked brand new. These he used on the newest discs. A closer look showed that a disc with an older sleeve had been moved toward the end of the collection, which was all wrong.

Without thinking, he slid it out and filed it away where it belonged. He took it out again to read the label. When did he take out his *Hopalong Cassidy* ET last? He couldn't remember, but he knew one thing for sure—he would never have filed it at the end of his collection, not a chance. It belonged where the 1949s were.

Someone got into his house while he was away. He grabbed the phone to call Stiles, dialed the first three numbers, and thought better of it. With no other evidence of a break-in, Stiles wouldn't be convinced with just a single disc moved out of its usual slot. And Tucker couldn't a hundred percent be sure that he didn't accidentally put it there himself. A misplaced disc and he jumped to the conclusion that there had been a second break-in?

He checked the front and back doors for any signs of tampering, but didn't have a clue what to look for. The utility room door that led out into his car port didn't show anything, either.

All the windows in the main part of the house were locked. The bedroom windows as well. Attached to the living room where the old back porch used to be was a closed in den that the previous owners added on before they sold. Above a couch littered with cushions against the far wall was a double-paned window.

During the cool nights of fall, Tucker and his wife opened it to let a breeze into the house.

A small metal arm acted as lock when pushed into a slot in the center section of the window. The arm was in the locked position. He pulled hard against the window to make sure it wouldn't open from sheer brute force. It didn't budge.

Okay, I'm losing it, he thought, as he climbed off the couch. On the other side of the window, his wife had hung a picture of them on their wedding day. Glowing in white, she gripped for dear life her new husband in the photo. They found it funny and she wanted it up in the den.

And at present it rested on its back on the floor.

In a panic, Tucker exited the house through the utility room. He opened the wood fence gate to look at the window from the back yard.

The only other time he could think of the picture being on the floor like that was when he slammed the window too hard, which rattled the wall and sent the precious photo to the floor. He may not have remembered moving the transcription disc, but he knew he hadn't touched that window in months.

He saw a tiny tear in the rubber seal where the outer window pressed against the inner window. On the other side of the seal was the metal lock arm. With a strong piece of steel someone could thread through the rubber seal against the arm and push it out of place, thus unlocking the window.

"But it's a tiny tear!" he said out loud.

He looked at it again. Still refusing to call Stiles, he knew for a fact that he'd been broken into. He also knew that if Stiles found out about it later, he would be a dead duck. If he had evidence of a break in, he should report it.

"Forget that," he said as he stormed back into the house.

He looked through the discs from first to last. Nothing else had been moved out of its proper place. He thumbed through the titles, hoping that one of them would jump out at him. Nothing did.

Planting himself in front of his computer in the study, Tucker typed in "Julia Appleton, University of Kansas," which turned up her page on KU's website. A phone number and e-mail address were both listed. Being Saturday, he decided on e-mail. Typing quickly, he outlined his relationship with Bobby, Bobby's death, and begged for any information she might have. He read through it twice before sending.

He prayed that she checked her work e-mail at home, or happened to be in the office that day. He felt urgency that he didn't back in Lincoln.

A sudden thought hit him: *Was Bobby's hit again?*

Tucker grabbed his car keys and cell phone, dialing Denise Ross as he left his house. She answered on the third ring and agreed to meet him there.

He threaded through the nearly deserted streets deftly. Saturday afternoons in Lyle were lazy, filled with walks at the high school track and a pick-up game of softball at the park. Everyone else either left town or hunkered down for the weekend to pass. Tucker broke the speed limit to get to Bobby's, which meant he only had to wait once he got there.

Resisting the temptation to commit a break-in himself, he found a stashed pack of cigs in his glove compartment. He lit up under the sturdy oak in front of Bobby's treasure house. As he inhaled his second draught of smoke, Tucker realized he hadn't lit up in over twenty-four hours. He had sucked down a couple in Lincoln, but that was it.

Had he really not had a cigarette in over a day-and-a-half?

He took a last drag from the newly lit cigarette and threw it away in the grass. He resolved to do away with the pack later. As he pressed down on the smoldering ember, Mrs. Ross pulled into the driveway.

"I don't want to go in there, Tucker," she projected over the running engine. "Are you sure there's been another break-in?"

"I don't know, Mrs. Ross. I just have a feeling."

"Well, go look and see."

He turned toward the door, but thought better of it. "Come with me."

"No, I'll stay here in the car."

"He would have wanted you to see his collection."

"I saw it plenty of times."

"Plenty of times?" he asked not believing her for a second.

"Once was enough."

"It's what Bobby loved in this life," he said. "I know it seems crazy, but it was his love. Come on, please."

"No."

"Denise, come on now; let's not be stubborn about it. He is your son."

She softened when he called her by her first name, a tactical maneuver on his part, and she killed the engine. He opened the door for her. She took the keys from him and opened the front door.

"This isn't going to be an easy thing for me, Tucker. You oughta know that." She hesitated on the front porch, peering through the diamond-shaped window set into the door. "He wasted his life away on his stuff."

"He didn't think so."

"I raised a hoarder," she said not holding back her grief. "He was a pack rat."

"He was expert in his field," Tucker countered.

"Says you."

"And dozens of others out there, believe you me."

She shook her long auburn locks as if warding off some unseen evil around her. She pointed to the door, which he opened, letting her in. A quick intake of air with a sigh following, Denise Ross bit her lip and punched the wall.

"Denise, come on, now."

She hit the wall again. "I'm mad, Tucker, can't you see that? Mad at him for all of this, mad at his father for setting him up with all that money when he died, and mad at me for not stopping it and making him live a normal life." One more punch into the wall and she was done.

"What can I say? Bobby lived in a world he created for himself and the rest of us just visited from time to time. He liked it that way. He was happy."

"He never married. He didn't have any children. What kind of life is that?"

"His own. I don't know what to say to make it any easier."

She waved at the shelves filled with his collections. "Well?"

"Oh, right."

He checked the house for any signs of a break-in. Checking every door and window and scrutinizing for any miniscule sign of tampering like he found at his house. He didn't find anything out of place or otherwise.

Denise joined him in the kitchen, the only room in the house not piled with Bobby's finds. She rummaged through the cabinets, drawers, and refrigerator before settling on brewing a cup of coffee in the maker.

"I should get over here and at least clear all this out," she said. "Any sign of a second attempt?"

"Not that I can tell."

"Should we call the police?" she asked while scooping out coffee grounds into the filter.

"No, forget it. I can help you clean the house out when you're ready."

"Why? You have your eye on something you want?" she shot back without thinking.

"I would never..." He let the thought fade. "I don't want one solitary thing from this house. I offered for your sake because this is going to be a chore for whoever has to do it. If you would rather find a reputable dealer, I can give you a few names. None of which have any connection with me to give me some kind of kickback." He stepped into the doorway of the kitchen. "I'll see you at the funeral." He turned to leave.

"Tucker, wait. I apologize. My big mouth eating my feet again. I'm sorry. Really, come here, sweetie." She pulled him to her hugging him close. No tears were spilled between them, but a gentle understanding grew.

The coffee maker beeped. She pushed away and poured them a couple of mugs. Adding cream and sugar to her own, she offered some to Tucker, who refused politely. They clinked the mugs together, blew the steam off, and sipped in silence.

"It's all yours, anyway, Tucker," Denise said.

"What are you talking about?"

She nodded toward the entrance. "All of that. Out there. It's all yours. I'm giving it to you as Bobby didn't have a will and he wanted it that way. And even if he didn't, I'm giving it to you and that's final. And not one word about it."

"Denise, no, please," he began.

"I said not one word. Bobby knew a lot of people in a lot of places, but he didn't have many friends. True friends in his life. You were one of them. My son was obsessed and that didn't bother you. It bothered me, but I'm his mother, I have the right to be bothered. I don't care what it's all worth, either. I want you to have it."

"Denise, let's just talk about it later. There's still so much to figure out," he pleaded.

"It won't change a thing. His father, God rest him, took care of both of us. Bobby spent his. I saved. One of our many differences."

He finished his coffee. She took the mug from him and rinsed it in the sink with care. She put it on the rack by the stove to dry.

"So no break-in then?" she asked again.

He thought of his transcription disc out of place back home. "Let me check out something right quick."

Tucker entered the room stacked with Bobby's ETs. No way in a million years would he ever consider them to be his, no matter if Denise bequeathed them to him or not. He feathered the sleeves with his fingertips as he walked along the shelving that held them all. Bobby worked hard to put this collection together. He had the eye, the knowledge, and the contacts.

What about that should concern me? Tucker asked himself as he inspected the room.

As he recalled, nothing had been taken from the room. Stiles and he had scanned the place top to bottom. But there were a couple of discs pulled out from their slots, which Bobby wouldn't do. Messier than Tucker, Bobby still valued order in the chaos of his treasure trove. He found the place again in the shelf. He pulled a few of the ETs out to check the labels.

Tucker found the two discs and slid them out to gander at the core labels again. "*I Love a Mystery,* Carlton E. Morse, 1949," Tucker read. "The New York revival run then," he said as an afterthought. He checked the discs shelved on either side of the ones he held his hand. These were the only *I Love a Mystery* discs in the lot. What had he missed?

"I need to get on back to the house, Tucker," Denise said from the doorway. "Anything?"

"More questions than answers. But no sign of a break-in here or anywhere else in the house."

"I still have a lot to do before the funeral next week," she admitted. She hugged him quickly and left.

Tucker pushed the two discs back in place on the shelf. He wanted to stay and just sit amongst Bobby's things to try and feel his presence, but without Bobby here to show off an item or two and express his passion, his love, for the precious things he found, it didn't mean much.

He locked the door behind him and left for home.

Chapter Thirteen

Take out Chinese, orange soda, popcorn, chased with half a cigarette and Tucker settled into his chair by the ancient stereo. He set up a mixed disc with *Fred Allen, Gunsmoke,* and *The Red Skelton Show* to pass the evening. Spinning the volume to "6," he leaned back in his recliner and shut his eyes to the world.

The episode of *Gunsmoke* balanced out the satirical humor of Fred Allen with Red Skelton offering clownishness to end his evening's listening on a high note. The radio version of *Gunsmoke* could be grim and serious, which never produced good dreams. He loved satire, but felt the strain in Allen's voice as he criticized intelligently the issues of the day. Skelton never failed with any of his outlandish characters.

As the credits to Skelton's show proclaimed the efficiency of Tide, Tucker took a bird's eye view of himself lying prone in his easy chair. Once a young man full of ambition to make the airwaves his frontier, his only goal now was to evaporate from daily cares, cease to exist. Beyond feeling sorry for himself after his wife's death, he didn't want to pursue much of anything anymore. What did it matter, anyway? All the stress invested in the problems of today ceased to matter a couple of years down the road, making it seem foolish to begin with.

Graying at the temples prematurely, Tucker envisioned his own future as the same isolated figure lying prostrate on his favorite chair still erasing himself from reality with the imagination of yesterday. With the lights dimmed in his house, the world dimmed as well, leaving him a lone listener in the dark. The voices of yesteryear, the sound effects of the foley artists, and the orchestras wove a tapestry of delight he experienced alone.

He believed with all his heart he had been born in the wrong time. The 1930s and 40s were his era. The clothes, the cars, the patriotism, and the entertainment were all things he loved about it. He truly belonged there. His nightly vigils by the light of the dial were more than just laughter, mirth, or wanting to see the bad guys hung. It transported him to a time when people seemed to actually care.

One week after his wife's death and the phone calls stopped, the food brought over ceased, and he was set adrift to deal with it all by himself. Family disappeared into the background unsure of what to say, in-laws forgot they had a son-in-law, and friends avoided him like he suddenly acquired a case of leprosy.

Wrapped in the folds of the past, he imagined the people different, dedicated to his grief, longing to get him back amongst the living.

The old radio shows did that for him. More than just a way to escape, they gave him somewhere to belong. He knew full well why Bobby hustled after the next "lost" show hidden in someone's basement untouched for decades. He understood the incessant desire to find meaning, even if that meant burrowing into the past. The shows did more than entertain, they opened up the consciousness of a generation. One that Bobby and Tucker could relate to much better.

Sad maybe, but the truth. They embraced the ideals of former days to get through and survive their own lives. And with Tucker's wife dead, it meant his only anchor to sanity.

Pondering the universe like this every night made Tucker's mind ache. Thoughts didn't bring people back. Surrounding one's self with the ornaments of the past didn't transport you there, not really. It offered a temporary fix to the here and now, which was way beyond repair.

Tucker rolled onto his side, shut out the invasive thoughts, and fell asleep.

The next morning brought sunshine, burnt coffee, and church. Tucker spruced up with a jacket, tie, and combed hair, which set his neighbors to take a second look. Casual with his attire and rarely a brush touching his head, Tucker needed a kick in his stride, thus the sharp clothes.

He paid attention during services, partook of communion, and put his check in the basket. Not exactly full of cheer, he put on the best face possible. Afterwards, a few passersby offered condolences. He searched for Denise but couldn't find her. She must have skipped.

"Tucker, I wanted to express my sorrow over Bobby's death," the pastor said. More than polite, the young man deeply felt every nuance of pain his congregation endured. Tucker would hear the same words, or some variation, dozens of times over the next few days, but none as sincere as from his pastor.

He thanked everyone for their thoughts and prayers, but secretly wished to be let alone so he could get to his car.

He dug for his keys and pressed the unlock button on the remote when a sleek Mercedes pulled up in front of him. He couldn't see inside for the tinted windows.

"I heard you were back in town," a familiar voice said as the passenger window slid down a crack. He could hear the tunes of KLMA playing at a tolerable level inside.

"Hey, Courtney, how are you?" he asked. The last one he thought to drive a car like this, he nevertheless was pleased to see his co-worker. With all that had happened the past few days, he hadn't thought about her much, but couldn't think of anyone else he would rather see at that very moment.

"I heard you were back in town and I figured you'd be doing the church thing this morning," she said. "Lunch and I'm buying." It wasn't a question or request.

"I think I've got a microwaveable box of linguini calling my name back at the house," he murmured.

"No, you don't. Come on, my treat."

"I really do have to get ready for my show tonight."

"I promise no Jackson hanging about," she said, all smiles.

"You sold me."

A plate of mozzarella sticks and two glasses of iced tea later, Tucker unwound his tie and loosened up. Something about Courtney eased his aching heart. Friendly from the first day she arrived, she tried hard to be a friend to Tucker. He did the polite thing and chitchatted about nothing in particular, avoiding any serious dialogue with her. He couldn't guess why.

"How was Nebraska?" she asked. She flagged the waiter down and asked for more tea.

"Did I tell you I was going to Nebraska?"

"Yeah, you said something about it in between takes of the Hibler Glass spot you were cutting the other day."

"It was confusing."

"Cornhuskers can be that way."

"They can?"

"Sure, I used to be one for a while, or I worked up there for a while."

"Where?"

"In a little town outside Lincoln. And then later on at a classic country station in Lincoln. But only for a little while."

"You never told me that."

"Is that where you went?" she asked. She tore open a packet of sweetener and stirred it into the tea.

"It is."

"Small world."

He didn't care for coincidence, not now anyway. She suddenly shows up to take him to lunch and mentions she worked in the very place where Bobby died? He shook it off, blaming himself of unwarranted suspicion. *She only wants conversation*, he thought.

She saw the perplexed look on his face.

"It's where your friend died, isn't it?"

"What is this, anyway?"

"I'm sorry?"

"Did you really work in Lincoln or are you jerking my chain?" he asked. Unwarranted or not, he couldn't stop himself.

"Yes, I did. What's wrong?"

He didn't answer, but instead stuffed his mouth with a mozzarella stick with sauce slathered on it.

"The station I worked for was owned by Monarch Communications, which owns half the stations in the country, Tucker," she explained. "I took a transfer in the company to Oklahoma because of a sick aunt, came across the Llama's radar, end of story." She took a sip from her tea. "And the interrogation, I hope."

"I wasn't..." he said, but couldn't finish. He was interrogating, but maybe she was, too.

"Okay, so I come on too strong. I've been accused of worse," she said. "I have done nothing but try to be nice to you and be your friend. You just won't have it. And I understand that. I really do whether you believe or not."

"Understand?"

She took a swig of tea. "At the risk of making you storm off in a huff, losing someone you love."

He nearly did storm away—and in a huff. They sat in silence for five minutes, each of them fiddling with the appetizers or their tea glasses. Not knowing what to say next, Tucker opened his mouth. Nothing came out. A wisp of a grin crossed her face.

"I had a good wife," he finally said ever-so quietly.

"I figured that. A little reading of past issues of the local paper confirmed it."

"I blame myself."

"We all do. Our loved one is dead and we're still living. Unfair doesn't seem to cover it. We feel responsible. You do. I did. It's the way we're made, I suppose. As hokey as it sounds I made a decision to live and just get on with it. This old life is a pain, but it's all we've got, as corny as that sounds. I saw your unhappiness, I related, I tried to reach out to you. It's as simple as that. No sinister motives. Nothing hidden up my sleeve. Just another person out here groping around trying to find someone, anyone to make a connection with because all the frozen linguini dinners in the world can't fill that hole." She took a deep breath. "And this is the most I've talked off the air in quite some time."

"Your aunt?" he asked. He took a long drink of iced tea. He felt his mouth drying out. Talking about this subject always did.

"Yes, my aunt."

"My wife." He didn't mean to make it sound like a challenge, but it did.

"Does she trump my aunt?"

"I'm not sure I really want to do this. And I'm not sure I want to do it with you, Courtney. No offense."

"And yet you're offensive," she said with a twinkle in her eye. "How about those Sooners?"

A little bubble of a laugh built in his chest, but only just. He raised his glass for a toast. She raised hers and they drank deeply. The entrees came right after, which saved them from needing to fill the air with constant conversation.

Bobby's death forced him to deal with a string of people he either wouldn't have, or avoided to save him the bother of attachment. Mose came closest to knowing, but thankfully, he saw him sporadically while stealing time for a smoke. Not extremely close to his own family or ex-in-laws, or however that worked, who gave him room to breathe after his wife's death.

And now, without pretense, this woman pushed her way into his life, had from the first day at the Llama, and made him speak. He didn't want it, but he knew he needed it.

"You ready for your show tonight?" she asked, shifting the conversation into safer ground.

"Yeah, I thought I would dedicate tonight's show to Bobby's favorites."

"Which are?"

"Oh, you wouldn't know them," he said.

"That's probably true. My musical knowledge doesn't go further back than Loverboy, so I'm sure I wouldn't know any of them." It was self-deprecating, but sure sounded that way to Tucker.

"Loverboy? 'Working for the weekend,' right? I'm sorry. I'm being a snob. Bobby loved *Bob and Ray, I Love a Mystery, Escape, Cavalcade of America,* and a bunch of others. Those were his mainstream loves, anyway. He really liked finding the obscure stuff, too, and enjoyed it."

"You're changing your line-up for Bobby, then?"

"You know about the line-up I announced last week?" he asked, amazed.

"Sure. That's pretty classy you doing that for him."

"Thanks."

"By the way, my granddad liked *Bob and Ray*," she said.

"Really?"

"Yes, really. I listened to a lot of what he had. Those guys were sharp."

"Yes, they were."

"And funny."

"And very funny."

"And *very* funny," she said.

"And I'm very sorry."

She swallowed a bite of her Dijon chicken. "I should apologize to you. I've been one of those desperate gals who are reaching out to anyone who will give her the time of day. It's tough making new friends when you're on the move all the time."

"There's Jackson," he teased.

"Be thankful I'm a lady, or I would fling rice at you," she chuckled.

"We're all really searching for a connection, aren't we?" he conceded. "Bobby, me, you, everyone. I had mine, and I'm sure you did as well with your aunt, and then…" He couldn't find the words to finish.

"Your voice is nice. It is on the air. That's what drew me to you in the first place. You have a great DJ voice."

"Not really."

"Okay, it stinks."

"Okay, wait a minute, so it's good already."

She laughed along with him, all wounds healed from their earlier conversation.

"I know that it's extremely intrusive of me, but could I sit in with you tonight at the station during your show?"

He didn't know what to say. A lump formed in the back of his throat. He retreated to his iced tea to mask his discomfort.

"I'll take that as a no," she said, disguising her disappointment.

"No, no," he countered. "I'm just…"

"Yeah, I can see that."

"It's just that I…"

"It's okay, forget I asked. I completely understand." She cut another slice of her chicken dish and put it carefully in her mouth. She pulled a strand of hair out of her mouth and shoved it over her ear.

Tucker still couldn't find anything to say to her request to sit with him during his show tonight. In his mind he planned it all out. Not sure of everything he would say, he knew that he wanted to do it alone. He desired to sit solo in the saddle tonight. But did he *need* to do that? She wasn't intruding. Was she?

"Funny thing about those old shows," she said out of the blue, "so many of them are lost to the vapor of the airwaves. Not everyone thought they were worth recording and saving for posterity."

"That's very true," he said, impressed with her bit of knowledge.

"And even if they recorded them, some stations would end up throwing them in the dumpster, anyway. It's a shame."

"Yeah, we have a lot of the shows, but there are so many that are long gone."

"Or, rumored about still existing somewhere," she said.

"That was Bobby's specialty."

"And I'm just throwing this out here, but I'm assuming you went to Lincoln because you thought what he was chasing got him killed."

"I don't really know, but it sure looks that way."

"Do the police believe that?"

"I've tried to convince them of that."

"And the break-ins are connected?"

He said they were. He told her about the second break-in at his house.

"So let me ask you something."

"Sure."

"If your friend died for a lost radio show, it begs the question: What show is worth protecting and killing for?"

"That's a loaded question, Courtney."

"Have you come up with an answer?"

"Nothing makes any sense to me."

"That's just it, isn't it? It doesn't have to make sense to you, Tucker. It has to make sense to the person out there willing to commit burglary here in Oklahoma, follow your friend to another state, and kill him."

"I can't think of anything."

"Well, take some advice. Quit looking at it through your eyes. Stop thinking with morals and ethics as your guide. This person who did this disregards both."

"It just seems silly almost to kill for a lost radio show."

"Pearls and gold come in many different forms, you know."

"You're right. You're absolutely right."

"I know," she said with a playful smile across her face.

"By the way, dinner is on me," he said, feeling a surge of confidence.

"I can go for that."

"You doing anything the rest of the afternoon?"

"How about I spend it with you?"
"My thought exactly."

Chapter Fourteen

At the radio station, things were quiet except for the automated computer satellite uplink that the station manager used for the weekends to save money. Tucker hated it as he thought it de-valued local radio, no matter what it cost. GMs everywhere boasted that uplinks saved barrels of money. Sadly, the personality of the station suffered from it as canned radio offered cookie-cutter DJs who presented universal, humorless quibble that didn't speak to the heart of the town.

Courtney rummaged in her office for a bit as Tucker begged a few minutes privacy as he prepped for Sunday's show, went through his stack of "to-dos," and answered any pressing e-mails. He still ignored the one from Stiles.

At the top of the inbox pile was an e-mail from Julia Appleton. She stated she knew Bobby well, hated to hear about his death, and would love to talk via Skype any chance that Tucker got. Looking at his watch, he decided now would work, so he logged into his Skype account and typed in Julia's user name that she provided. Barely knowing the Skype date protocol, Tucker did know that he should send a typed message first. Thankfully, she was online, so he tapped out a quick hello message.

"Be ready in a sec," came the reply.

He jotted down a few questions he thought were relevant. Just like anything involving Bobby, questions begat more questions. Bobby couldn't be tracked in a straight line. He swerved and veered with every new piece of information.

The computer rang at him as Julia Appleton sent an invitation to chat face to face with him. He accepted and waited for the audio and screen image to get set up. At least the GM of the station forked out the necessary cash for quick Wi-Fi.

An aged face with silky auburn hair came into focus. He could just make out the beginnings of silvery gray looping through the strands of her hair. Hazel eyes twinkling with playfulness blinked repeatedly at him. She was another webcam user who spent more time looking at herself on screen, just like he did. A warm smile spread evenly as she sized Tucker up from hundreds of miles away.

"Greetings and salutations," she said with honey-dipped vowels. *Not a native Kansan*, Tucker thought immediately. She seemed to read his thoughts. "I'm a displaced Alabaman in the land of the wheat field."

"I'm Tucker Niles and a good friend of Bobby's."

"Ah, you must be playing Sherlock Holmes," she said. "Which version? The films with Rathbone, or the radio show?"

"Need you ask."

She laughed at that. "Olay, so Rathbone played in both. It was Anthony Boucher who made the difference."

"You're so right," Tucker said. "His radio scripts were top notch. So Bobby?"

"Yeah, I've heard of you. He mentioned you a couple of times in passing."

"You knew him, how?" he asked pulling his attention off the square with his face in it to watch her. He stared directly into her eyes. Using a webcam made it so much easier to do.

"Your friend Bobby is...*was* a hound dog, and I don't mean after the ladies. Although if I were twenty years younger, I would have put on my best flirt," she said. Sensing her playfulness, Tucker decided to join in.

"He wouldn't know a woman if she came up and kissed him right on the mouth," he said, knowing it to be true. "I don't think he knew where he was half the time."

"Oh, yes, he did, honey," she said tapping her head. "He lived right here. This was his own personal wonderland."

"That may be what got him killed."

"The academic in me says that's absurd and that you're wasting your time and let the police find the maniac who did this. The paranoid conspiracy theorist is right along with you."

"What was he working on when you met him?"

"Well, to shine my own trophies for a minute, which all good professors do any chance we get, I teach audio production, among other mass comm-related classes here at KU." She sipped from a glass of something dark on her desk. For all Tucker knew, it could be bourbon and Coke with this woman's devil-may-care attitude. "I'm also a historian, which is more a curse than blessing as you realize what idiots the human race is. However, not to digress too much, I have written quite a few articles dealing with audio history and have been working on a book as well."

"About what?"

"Do you want the whole pretentious title, or would a two-cent version do?" she asked.

"Pick one."

"I'm looking at women and their role in the early years of broadcasting in Kansas City. You should hear the title I'm gonna use to publish it under. Sheesh!

Sometimes I wish I was back in the land of cotton," she said, all smiles.

Tucker caught on pretty quick to her "aw, shucks" routine, which she put on full throttle. She used it as a device; a way to pull the other person out of his shell without revealing anything important from her side of the court.

"When did Bobby enter your life?"

"A year ago."

He waited. So did she.

Tucker relented. "Okay, how about I tell you a story, Miss Appleton."

"It's Missus, but you can call me Julia. I like your face."

"I like your patter," he said, laughing as he did so. "It suits you."

"I wish the administration agreed with you. I'm all ears, believe it or not, for your story."

Tucker started with the week before and Bobby's visit to the station, his mysterious trip to Nebraska, his odd lines of inquiry, and the senselessness of his death over something so trivial. He left nothing out. Not that he trusted her, he felt the urgency to get at the heart of the matter. If darker forces still loomed out there, they took aim at him now.

Realizing this for the first time, he broke out in goose bumps, even though his office was warm. The second break-in meant he was a serious target. And with nothing found he knew hidden eyes were watching him.

He finished by telling Julia about his second trip to Bobby's house to look at the transcription disc collection. She soaked it up without commenting. She drained her glass dry, poured the remains of a generic soda, dug in her desk for a flask, and poured the contents in the cup. Tucker guessed right.

"Don't tell anyone," she said, shushing him with a cantankerous finger brushing her lips. "All good professors are boozers or are on some kind of narcotic. It's what separates us from the herd."

"It's your turn, Julia," he challenged.

"I like stories that start with 'once upon a time,'" she whispered.

"I like those kind of stories."

"They make everything safe in a way. I don't know why."

He shot her a quizzical look.

"It's because those stories have nothing to do with life, real life, that is. My field of interest fascinates me, not because of how wonderful audio is, which it is, but because it was pioneered by a bunch of rogues, bandits, and outlaws. Its history is filled with charlatans, conjurers, and slight-of-hand men."

"Like Orson Welles," he added.

"He was the king of them all, surely," she agreed. "But it goes back even further to Lee DeForest, who thought he created the airwaves single-handedly. But I do go on, don't I? I keep thinking you're a student and there will be a quiz on Monday." She giggled harshly, washing it down with a stiff drink from her glass.

"And you write about that side of radio history?"

"Audio, dear, audio," she corrected. "If you're going to sound more important than you are, you have to learn all the pretentious terms."

"All right, audio."

"Bobby Ross popped into my life as yet another chapter in *radio's* history," she said with a wicked wink. "A year ago he read an article I wrote about the stacks of missing transcription discs that seemed to have been snuffed out of existence. Most of your audio historians blame it on station owners who could care less, clumsy operators, and dozens of other reasons that are very plausible. In fact, that's what happened to many of them."

"I sense a 'but' coming just about now," he said.

"Now honey, did I interrupt your fascinating story?"

"No, ma'am."

"Then be so kind as to offer me the same courtesy."

"I'll do it." He mimed zipping his lip. She toasted the gesture with another drink. If she felt any effects, Tucker didn't see it.

"The one element that most historians refuse to acknowledge, because they're idiots, is the collector. Radio shows were viewed as being disposable, a one-time event that got recorded for every other reason but the purpose of posterity. But there were a few who instantly saw the potential for future rewards and got every available disc they could get their hands on. There were people scrounging around for ETs before anyone thought they might matter twenty years down the road. And those collectors who had money snatched up not just a few shows here and there, but tens of thousands of them. So many, in fact, that they had to build special rooms to hold their collections."

"You're talking about people like Robert Bellevue," he said, unable to contain his excitement. Julia could tell a ripping yarn and he got caught up in it. "Sorry, sorry," he apologized.

"You're fine. So, you've come across the infamous Robert Bellevue, the oil man," she said.

"Only because Bobby did."

"Bobby heard about him a year ago. How? I'm not completely sure, but I'm guessing through some old-time radio trader who deals in rumors and gossip."

"Probably true. Most of them like to spin their own stories to add to the mystique of the medium."

"And rightly so. Audio is almost a mystical thing," she conceded. "Bellevue was just barely alive when I interviewed him."

Tucker nearly fell out of his chair. "You interviewed him?"

"Don't go thinking you've found the mother lode, Tucker. At the end of his life that man was ornery just because he could be. I was young and looking for a nugget of information for my next article so I could tick that off the administration's list of things I was supposed to do so they'd keep me another year."

"The word is he had a huge collection."

"He did have. I saw it. And he was one that built a wing onto his house to accommodate all of it."

"Did he let you listen to any of them?" he asked, letting his greediness show.

"He showed me a lot of discs that were very rare. As a matter of fact, at the time I thought he might've had the only remaining copies of some shows." She took a thoughtful drink nearly finishing it. "He played snippets of a few of them, but never a complete show. He had every piece of equipment imaginable, too. But really, all the man wanted was to get me in the sack."

"You're kidding."

"Does this face look like it could kid?" she asked. Ever the joker, Tucker wondered if she got serious.

"What did his wife say?"

"She was right there when he did it. It was some kind of game for him. The perv. But I went along with it to get my info so I could type twenty pages of drivel that would get read by four other academics out there in the world who actually cared."

"Did you ever see him again?" he asked.

A gentle knock came at the door. He held up a finger to Julia. Courtney eased into the room quietly. She mouthed if it was okay for her to be there. He waved her to sit down. Julia waved at her.

"Hi, honey, I'm Julia Appleton and I'm flirting with your boyfriend," she said as way of introduction.

"He's not..."Courtney said, but got interrupted.

"We're talking about ancient history, but I promise it won't be on the test," Julia said. "Where were we, Tucker?"

"Bellevue's widow?" he asked again.

"Oh yeah. No, didn't see him this side of eternity. I did see his widow, though a couple of years later."

"When was that?"

"Right when the trading of reel-to-reel tapes of old radio got going pretty steady. You know, it was just like anything else, a few collectors found each other and they started networking. It took longer with rotary dial phones and actual letters, but they found each other."

"When the shows got circulating and the trade really started," he added.

"That's right. I wanted to talk to those folks and get their take on it. They didn't have the dough that the Bellevues of this world have, which offered a different perspective on the hobby. She was there at one of them. I can't remember where. She thought the whole thing was silly."

"Why's that?"

"Honey, listen, those folks were trading a handful of shows here and there. They didn't have tens of thousands in their collections like many collectors do with the mp3s. They worked hard for every episode they got. Her husband owned the biggest slice of anyone in that room," she said.

"It was a contest then? To make sure he was still top dog?"

"Something like that."

"So I'm trying to play six degrees of Bobby Ross here, Julia, but I'm coming up with nothing."

"Bobby found the widow."

Courtney leaned forward suddenly interested in the threads of the tale. Tucker found her curiosity—dare he think it?—attractive. He didn't have the time or inclination to ponder those dark waters. He returned his attention back to Julia.

"She's still alive?"

"She's like the cat with nine lives," Julia said. "That lady has gone through cancer, a heart attack, and the first signs of dementia."

"Bobby got to see the collection then?" Tucker asked jumping to conclusions to get Julia to tell her story faster.

"The collection is gone, Tucker."

"What's that mean?"

"Just what I said, it's long gone."

Courtney opened a soda for him as he sucked hungrily on a cigarette. She wrinkled her nose as a whiff of smoke blew into her face. He shrugged as a way of apology, but she fanned with her hand in front of her nose.

"I think I can kick it," he said meaning every word of it.

"For me it was food."

"What are talking about?"

"The grief."

"We're back to that again," he said as a lungful of smoke burned inside.

"My aunt's favorites, too. Pecan pie with a splash of whisky, but in my case a shot or two, and homemade chocolate cake, and butterscotch pudding."

"Your aunt liked desserts."

She laughed. "She did. And that woman never gained so much as a pound. Me? I put on twenty in a month and a half. Well, that tore it and I got on a treadmill and quit the desserts, aunt or no aunt," she said.

"This is your way of telling me that I will quit smoking?" he asked her, intrigued with her answer.

"Either you will, or you won't."

"That's great advice," he groaned, not meaning any sarcasm.

She plunged ahead. "I'm the best kind of weatherman. I don't go for all these percentages of how much it will rain. Either it will, or it won't. You'll either quit or you won't. You'll either get over it, or you won't."

"Won't," he said in unison. "Yeah, yeah, I know. The choir is singing, Courtney, but we're not listening to the words of the song."

"I like that analogy."

"Came right off the top of my head," he admitted with a toothy grin.

"I'll bet." She moved to the top step of the entrance to the station and sat down. "Are you going to explain what in the world that woman was talking about?"

"I'm not sure if I can fathom it all myself. Putting it simply, a rich eccentric bought a bunch of transcription discs of old shows, brags about his collection, but like the rest of us, he kicks the bucket."

"Nicely put."

"The widow, who is still living, but is now a recluse doesn't have the collection anymore in the house, which may be the key."

"Meaning, you think she still has it."

"Meaning, that a lot of folks like Bobby think she still has it. In a warehouse, probably, or some storage facility somewhere. The main thing is that others got to her long before Bobby did."

"This Tony Boucher, who is he in all of this?"

"An enigma, to say the very least."

"I don't understand what's going on," she said matter-of-factly. "I'm just along for the ride."

"Tony is short for Anthony," he explained.

"Okay, Anthony Boucher."

"It's a false name," he explained further. "Anthony Boucher was a science fiction and mystery writer. He died back in '68."

"What's he have to do with this?"

"I think it's someone's idea of a joke. Boucher also wrote for radio for a few years. He scripted *The Adventures of Ellery Queen* and *Sherlock Holmes*. The guy should've called himself "Mr. E" if he thought he was that clever."

"I take it this is an in-joke to other radio show collectors?" she inquired putting the pieces together on her own.

"Any old time radio fan would know Boucher's name. In his day he was pretty well known in mystery circles. He also helped create Mystery Writers of America."

"So whoever this person is, he's thumbing his nose at the rest of the collecting community."

"That's about right. When I first got involved in collecting, there were complaints about a collector they referred to as "A.B.," along with carefully chosen adjectives, who bragged about his own transcription discs collection. He also didn't have any scruples about how he got his shows, including thievery."

"And according to your professor friend, Bobby tracked down this "A.B." person and said he would confront him about some long-lost shows that should be shared with the rest of the collector community."

"And the rest of the world, which would have been Bobby's way of looking at it," he said. He couldn't hide his sadness. "If the shows were moved, or 'long gone,' as Julia put it, then our mysterious Boucher had to work very hard to find them and steal what he could get his hands on."

"And Bobby found him?"

"You heard Julia. She didn't know. But she said Bobby thought he found him."

"This is getting scary now," Courtney said softly. "I'm craving a piece of pie all the sudden."

"I'm thinking about another smoke."

"Tucker."

"Only kidding."

"But he never said anything to you?" she asked, hardly believing it.

"Nope. Just the cryptic videos, but I've watched them and there's nothing encoded in them, or backward masking, or whatever weird thing you can think of," he said offhandedly. "That would be Bobby's style if he could figure out a way to do it."

"The frightening question is would this Boucher kill to protect what he supposedly stole?"

"That's the only explanation I've got right now."

"And no one knows who this guy really is?"

"You heard Julia. He's near mythic proportions now so it would have to be someone who knows him or have firsthand knowledge of him," he said.

"Do you call the police with any of this?"

"I'm not sure how far it would fly as far-fetched as it is. I haven't talked to Detective Stiles since I got back."

"He came by the station while you were away. I don't know what he wanted. He wouldn't say."

"Funny, he hasn't called."

"Do you even have your cell phone on you?" she asked, neatly patting him down as if being frisked in airport security.

"Hey now," he chuckled fending her off. "Watch yourself there."

She opened the back door to the station and shuffled him indoors. "Maybe it was important, Tucker, what Stiles wanted. You never know."

Tucker snapped his fingers with one hand while gently bopping his forehead with the other.

"What now?" Courtney asked gearing up for the next revelation.

"He did send me and e-mail, but I've been ignoring it. He chapped me last time I talked to him, so I've been giving the cold shoulder treatment."

"Remind me to never get on your bad side. Do you pout, too?" She playfully punched him on the arm. Without thinking, he feinted to the left drawing her attention, and then pulled on a strand of her hair. It didn't hurt, but she retaliated by tickling his ribs. He countered by pinning her arms to wall of the hallway. They stood like that for a moment too long.

Their lips met before either one of them could think of a reason not to. Tucker hadn't kissed another woman since his wife and the warmth of Courtney's mouth nearly engulfed him. Exploratory in nature, the kiss meant more than that for each of them. Courtney, to fill a void in her life, and Tucker to see if he still existed amongst the living. But just as soon as she moved her arms to his waist to hold him close, Tucker stood back taking in a deep breath. He couldn't move, couldn't speak, and didn't know what to say.

"I'm sorry," Courtney said breaking the spell of the moment. "I'll stay in my corner from now on. That was way out of line and I shouldn't have done that."

She walked briskly down the hall into her office shutting the door behind her. Tucker didn't dare stop her as he wouldn't know what to do anyway. Images of his wife filled his mind. Guilt prodded him into his office. He plopped down in his chair replaying the kiss over on the movie screen in his brain. He liked it. He liked Courtney.

But how do you comprehend feelings of guilt? It drove his every waking moment. He would have been the one driving the car if he'd stepped away from the job and given her the support and attention she so justly deserved. He transferred his affection to Bobby, who died as well. He knew he couldn't take blame for that, but he realized that he needed to track down his friend's final days to discover the truth.

And Courtney? She kept knocking on a closed door hoping for it to crack open. Just as she said, from day one she attempted to get to know him. The Jackson Mulroys of this world didn't appeal to her. She wanted to befriend a geeky hermit who lived within the airwaves of his radio. Knowing it a cliché to say he couldn't and shouldn't because of the memory of his wife, he wouldn't allow that to enter his head.

Instead, he chalked it up to an intense loneliness that he felt he deserved. He could take self-loathing to new heights if he allowed himself the melancholy, so he turned his thoughts elsewhere.

Wasn't there something about an e-mail? He scanned quickly through the mounting list of unanswered e-mails in his inbox. Finding Stiles' message, he clicked it open.

"Tracking the money side of things. Only small amounts on Bobby's c.c. Did he deal in cash only with bigger purchases? Call me. –Stiles"

Tucker hadn't considered the money trail. He wasn't surprised that Stiles couldn't find one as Bobby did like to deal in cash for most things. His credit card he liked to use for meals, clothes, and daily needs like parking or a coffee or…

He nearly fell backward out of his chair reaching for his cell phone. Dialing frantically, he couldn't believe he hadn't made the jump. He spent all this time tracking Bobby's steps, who he talked to, what he was after. What if he found it already? Sure, he and Stiles and others who knew Bobby played that scenario, but not in a practical sense.

What if Bobby found his holy grail? And what if he knew someone very dangerous was about to kill him because of it?

The phone rang repeatedly.

"Come on, come on," he mumbled.

Stiles answered on the fourth ring. "Hello, stranger. You decided to call."

"I just opened your e-mail. I'm a bit behind."

"How was Nebraska?" Stiles asked.

"Question for you," Tucker said ignoring him.

"What's that?"

"The credit card transactions."

"What are you talking about?"

"Of Bobby's. Are you awake or were you on a Twinkie coma?"

Tucker heard Stiles moving around on the other end. "Very funny. Okay, credit card of Bobby's. Mainly small stuff like I said in my e-mail."

"Did he ship anything?" Tucker asked.

"How am I supposed to know? We were looking for big payments. Something that was worth a lot. I don't know if he did, or not," Stiles admitted.

"You need to find out for me," Tucker ordered.

"You want fries with that, too," Stiles shot back.

"If I said it was important, would you believe me?"

A slight hesitation came from the other end. "I don't have any of that stuff here with me. It's at the office."

"So you were in a Twinkie coma," Tucker gibed.

"Not on your life, man. Try Little Debbies. Stay by your phone." The phone went dead on the other end.

Tucker stood up collecting his thoughts from the very beginning. Like a DVD player he scanned backwards replaying scenes from the past week. He would pause a moment recollecting what was said. He put all the scraps together to look at the whole picture.

"Gotta have a smoke," he murmured as he grabbed his pack off the desk. He ignored Courtney's door as he sped to the rear entrance.

At the back door he nearly ran over Mose who had his key outstretched for the knob. Mose stepped back as quick as he could, but caught the edge of the door on the palms of his hands.

"Whoa, Nelly," he said.

"Mose! Sorry. Are you okay? Did I get you?"

"Where's the fire?"

Tucker lit up. "I wish in my mind."

"Trying to figure things out, huh?" Mose asked. He lit up using Tucker's lighter.

"I feel so dense right now about my friend and his death. I have a few bits and pieces, but can't make any sense out of any of it."

"Bobby Ross?"

"Yeah. He liked being cryptic with nearly everything he did. In life it helped pass the time, but in death it's driving me crazy." Tucker sucked hard on the filter drawing in as much smoke as his lungs could hold.

"I knew his momma," Mose said through a puff of silky smoke.

"I didn't know that. When?"

"They used to live next door to us on the south side of town."

Tucker knew the code word for "the other side of the tracks" in Lyle. It was the south side. He didn't know Denise came from there. He admitted it to Mose.

"She and her family worked real hard, but couldn't get on their feet for something happening. Her momma got sick and then her sister. Then her daddy lost part of his leg in Korea. Just one thing after another." Mose shook his head remembering it.

"And then she married up and out of there," Tucker said.

"That she did, but she still owns that house. You know that?"

"No, I didn't."

"She used to take Bobby down there all the time when he was younger. She wanted him to see where she'd come from, make him appreciate what his daddy gave him," Mose said. He spoke methodically, carefully not condemning or judging.

"He did eventually."

"I'm sure he did."

"He was forever chasing after something, though. His feet couldn't stand still. He was all the time restless."

"Like you?"

Tucker smashed the ember of the cigarette with his toe. He let the smoke drift from his mouth on its own. Who did he equate Mose to in his life? Andy, from *Amos and Andy,* with so much wisdom? Could be.

The six degrees of Bobby Ross haunted him now as nearly everyone he'd been in contact with had some connection to him, even Mose.

"I don't guess I was always this way," Tucker answered after a short eternity.

"It's always that way when the pathway you've chosen for yourself doesn't work out right. We all know about that at some time or another."

"I'm jittery I guess because I want to understand why every little thing happens. And don't tell me there's a reason, either. I've heard that 'til I can't take it anymore," Tucker said.

"Ah, it's not for us to know about all the reasons, Tucker. We're too simple for that. But listen up, sometimes the mystery is half the joy of it. If everything could be understood, then why get up every morning and go through our lousy routines? If we had it all figured out, where would be the wonder and the curiosity? I know I'm soundin' like one of them Hallmark cards now, but think about it. We're all so confused about the mystery of life and think we need to figure it all out. Me, I love a mystery. It's what keeps me going after all these years."

Tucker's eyebrows shot as high as they could go. He repeated the snap/slap he did earlier.

"Am I the idiot!" he exclaimed to the blue sky. He stormed back into the station.

"What'd I say?" Mose asked no one.

PART THREE

RADIO GENTLEMEN: THE LIFE AND TIMES OF TUCKER NILES Episode #24

MUSIC: THEME. WAGNER PIECE.

ANNOUNCER: We return now to *Radio Gentlemen: The Life and Times of Tucker Niles.*

MUSIC: THEME BUILDS, THEN OUT.

ANNOUNCER: Tucker Niles has more questions than answers about the murder of his friend, Bobby Ross. Intrigue, mystery, and a possible love interest have crept into Tucker's life.

SFX: FOOTSTEPS ON CONCRETE.

ANNOUNCER: Will he see another tomorrow?

MUSIC: THEME. SUBDUED/DARK.

SFX: A BLAZING FIRE

SFX: A SCREAMING SIREN IN DISTANCE

ANNOUNCER: Join us find out...in today's episode of *Tucker Niles*!

SFX: A CAR DRIVING FAST ON HIGHWAY

TUCKER: (voice over narration) Putting my foot in my mouth and my heart out my sleeve has been a long-time practice of mine. And apologies are hard and don't come cheap in this faithless world...

Chapter Fifteen

Tucker refreshed his knowledge on the internet for the next hour. Forgetting his upcoming broadcast, he concentrated on every factoid he could find. He re-read entries on his dog-eared copy of his old time radio encyclopedia written by John Dunning. He cross-referenced a couple of other books on the subject before he called it quits.

If he knew how to pay attention, he would have figured this out days earlier. In a flight of fancy, he picked up his cell phone to call Dave or Rhonda to let them know. Cycling through his list of contacts, he put the phone back in his pocket without calling. Better not stir up intrigue until he could prove it—best for him to keep things on the QT.

He fired off another invitation for Julia Appleton to Skype again as he needed to ask a couple of questions. She wasn't online and he had gotten get a phone number from her. He typed an e-mail to her instead. If he needed to, he could check for her answer on his cell phone. Tucker brainstormed for anything else he could do, but nothing came.

He should talk to Courtney.

Reluctantly, he traipsed down the hallway lingering outside her door for an age. Too much emotion made him kiss her. He knew it to be the truth. His wife accused him of his impulsiveness that could get him into trouble, and often did with her.

Naturally, the one person who gave comfort through her loss was Bobby. He could say the right thing at the exact time Tucker needed it. He would be silly when all seemed lost. And he would sit up with Tucker and listen to radio shows until dawn. But he also warned Tucker about "wallowing in it for too long," or he could be a casualty, too. Maybe not in the literal sense, but another of life's zombies that strolled around dopey-eyed and lost without any hope for a much-improved tomorrow.

"Not now," Tucker whispered. He rapped on the door. No answer came. He peeked through the door and no Courtney. "Great, she's gone."

He lumbered around the corner near the broadcasting studio. Through the glass window, he saw Courtney sitting in the saddle bobbing her head to the unidentifiable classic rock tune playing on the Llama. The GM liked the broadcast to thrum in the background in the front offices and lobby, but Tucker could rarely make out the artist, he had it playing so low.

Tucker watched her, asking himself why she picked this particular time to push hard into his life. Sure, he recognized gentle advances, but today of all days she got the door open. Beyond his fear, his paranoia brought on by the last week's events kicked his apprehension up a notch.

Courtney opened her eyes as the song finished, caught him staring, and presented her best "mock" beauty queen wave. He returned it and walked to the studio door. She spun the chair around to face him.

"I love radio," she admitted. "The corporate stuff is for the birds, but even it has some redeeming qualities."

"Name one," he teased.

"The music, for one," she said without missing a beat.

"There is that." He dared not confront the kiss in the hallway, but let it alone for another time.

"Are you ready for your show tonight?" she asked to keep the conversation flowing.

He opened up his mouth to answer when his cell phone went off. Courtney chuckled at his *Shadow* ringtone warning that "the weed of crime bears bitter fruit." Before it could finish the famous phrase, he punched a button.

"What did you find?" he asked Stiles.

"And hello to you, too."

"Did he?"

"Yes, he did."

Tucker nearly jumped for joy. "Where to?"

"Where to what?" Stiles asked. His voice echoing in the hall outside the studio. Courtney came over to listen. "Oh, the package he mailed. I don't know. Have you gotten anything from him?"

"Wouldn't I tell you if I did?"

"I don't know. Would you?" Stiles shot back.

Tucker ignored him. "Great. Another dead end."

"Hold on just a sec. I'm sure we can get a trace on the package tomorrow when the post office opens up in Lincoln."

"So he mailed it from Lincoln?" Tucker asked.

"Yep, from the branch in downtown."

"Downtown?"

"Yes. It must have been a pretty good sized package, too. He spent a little over thirty dollars to send it off."

"And that figure didn't catch your attention?"

"Not when I was looking for something in the thousands, Tucker," Stiles snapped.

"Okay, you said that already. It's just so frustrating to be so close."

"You should be on this end of it. I have a murder to solve."

Courtney threw in: "What about his mother?"

"I saw her yesterday and she didn't mention getting anything from Bobby," Tucker said.

"What's that?" Stiles asked confused with the seemingly unconnected information.

"Answering a question. Hold on." He put a thumb over his phone.

"Did he use a post office box?" Courtney asked. "That would protect his privacy to a certain extent."

"If he did, he sure didn't tell me. But that's not surprising."

"Tucker, you there?" Stiles interrupted. "Hello, anyone at home? I'm talking to myself now, aren't I?"

"Would his mother know about that, ya think?" Courtney said.

"It's possible, but you just never know with Bobby."

"It's all I can think of, Tucker."

"Tucker! Earth is calling!" Stiles yelled from the phone.

"That has to be it, Courtney," Tucker said as he removed his thumb from the phone.

Stiles and Tucker said in unison: "A post office box."

"In Lyle?"

"No, Puskatahaw. Can you explain that to me when we have a perfectly good post office here in town?"

"That's Bobby being protective. That has to be where he shipped it," Tucker said.

"It? Do you know what *it* is?"

Tucker ignored him. "What about a key?"

"That was my next question to you. He didn't have any keys on him when he...was found."

Tucker nearly slung the phone away out of sheer frustration. Okay, yes, Bobby had been there for him, but that didn't change the fact that he could be the most enigmatic person on the face of the earth. His frown deepened.

"Is it worth losing your cool over?" Courtney asked. He barely heard her. She said it again.

"Yes, very much so."

"Tucker?" Stiles' voice crooned from the speaker on the phone.

"Let me call you back." Tucker slipped the cell phone back into his pocket. The craving for another cigarette hit him like a pressing weight. Not a physical need, but a deeply rooted psychological one. The urge overwhelmed him.

"I need a smoke," he said as he spun on his heel toward the back entrance.

Courtney tried to grab him. "Wait a minute, hold on. Tucker!"

"I don't know why I'm doing this in the first place," he exclaimed. "If he was here, I'd lay him out cold!"

"No, you wouldn't."

"Oh yes, I would."

"No. You. Would. Not." She stopped him just short of the back exit.

"I'll do a lot better with nicotine."

"Let me ask you something. Do you think Bobby knew he was in trouble up there? Do you think he knew someone was after him? Someone that would kill him? Do you think he suspected anything?"

"Honestly, I don't know."

"Guess then."

He exhaled loudly not hiding his aggravation from her. If she didn't run off after seeing this side of him, she never would leave him alone, he thought miserably.

"Looking back at everything, the videos, all the people he talked to, the violent way he died, I would have to say he would've been blind not to see the danger. So, for the sake of argument, I'll say he did."

"What was more important to him?"

"What do you mean?" he asked not following her line of reasoning.

"His life or whatever he chased?"

"That was Bobby all over. He'd do that, yeah."

"So if he shipped whatever it was he found to a post office twenty minutes down the road from here, what was his failsafe? Would he let it sit there forever?"

"No way. He would make sure someone would get it."

"Who, Tucker?"

He looked at her knowing the answer. "Me."

"Now we're getting somewhere, don't you think?"

"I still need that smoke."

"Hold on now. He didn't tell you in those videos he sent you?"

"No."

"And no phone calls."

"No, even though he promised to call, he didn't."

"And he didn't come and see you before he left town?" she asked.

"He came and saw me last week at the station, but we just drove around town listening to some obscure show he likes."

He nearly repeated the snap/slap as he ran past her into the parking lot.

Tucker nearly peeled out into the street next to the radio station. He slammed the brakes hard at the stop light jerked both he and Courtney against the seat belts. He dialed Stiles on his cell phone.

"Meet me at the Puskatahaw post office," he said without waiting for an answer before hanging up.

"I hope this isn't *Death Race 2000*," Courtney joked.

"Sorry, I didn't realize I was driving like a maniac."

"That's what I'm here for."

"Somebody needs to be."

He eased through the green light before pushing past the speed limit. If he got pulled over, he hoped Stiles would vouch for him.

"I think that's clever of him hiding the key in your ashtray. I think maybe he was telling you something."

"You think so?"

"I do."

"Me, too, the bum," he said with the first genuine smile of the day.

"Does that mean he thought he was in trouble when he left?" she asked.

"Probably so. He knew how the wind blew with other collectors and those in the trade. I'm guessing he thought he might be getting in over his head."

"But he went anyway."

"He kept calling it the 'holy grail' the night he came to see me. That wasn't something he would throw around lightly. Shipping it to me without telling me was his way of protecting the find."

"Do you know what that is?"

"I do, actually. It took me a while, but it's been there all along. An *uber* collector like Bobby would have spotted it in a New York minute, but I'm a little slow on the uptake. It took Mose telling me how much he loved life's mysteries to make it all fall into place."

"I don't understand."

"Let me tell you a story."

Chapter Sixteen

"A guy by the name of Carlton E. Morse who got into radio in its early days became a writer and director of programming pretty early in his career. He wrote all kinds of stuff—serials, adventure stories, and a long-running show called *One Man's Family* that was basically a slice-of-life soap opera, which was extremely popular. His work was respected in the budding medium.

"In early '39 he started a serial adventure story that also became popular, mainly with juvies, but with other folks, too. He called it *I Love a Mystery* and filled it with enough blood and thunder to scare the most hardened of teenager. It was the Three Musketeers of its day with a group solving mysteries, fighting crime, and even facing what appeared to be supernatural trouble. The show was a fifteen-minute daily serial for a while, but was done in different formats later on.

"The characters were Jack, Doc, and Reggie who served in China's war against Japan; that's where they met, and later formed the A-1 Detective Agency in Hollywood after they got back to the states.

"That should've been the big tip-off for me with Bellevue calling his oil company the A-1, but I was slow on the uptake. If I'd paid attention earlier at Bobby's house with the break-in, I would have noticed the two ETs that were pulled out of their slot—the *I Love a Mystery* discs Bobby had. Same thing at my house with my collection, except the burglar thought I kept mine in alphabetical, too, which I don't.

"Any-who, Morse had his adventurers traveling all over the globe righting wrongs, but they weren't the best of fellahs, meaning they broke the law and bent the rules to see justice done. When the actor who played Reggie committed suicide, Morse wrote him out of the story, replacing him with a secretary named Jerry Booker. They searched for lost loot, visited exotic places, and had every conceivable adventure you could dream up, or Morse could dream up.

"That show ran for a few years on the west coast and then in the late forties, early fifties with a New York run, which is where the majority of the surviving shows come from. You see, that's the kicker to all this. There are only fragments, which is one chapter out of the serial, most with bad quality audio, and a few of the thirty minute shows, from the Hollywood run.

"This is the run that the fans and collectors prize the most as they believe the New York run is inferior in every aspect. But here's the thing: supposedly there were transcription discs for most, if not all, of the Hollywood run that Morse had, or was supposed to have. And when the trade got going full blast, guess which show everyone wanted? So the search began by rabid fans all over with fragments found hither and yon, but no complete chapters for any of the serials from the west coast series.

"And that's how legends and myths are born. A guy by the name of Jim Harmon, a big fan of the show, befriended Morse after the radio hey-day and asked him where all the discs were. Morse didn't know. That's how the story goes, anyway. And then rumors spread about missing shows being hoarded somewhere by some miser who wouldn't share his treasure trove with the rest of the fans.

"The show certainly isn't the greatest that radio offered, but it is the most sought after with a fragment here and there showing up. This restarts the interest in finding the missing shows, which in turn adds another chapter to the legend. Bobby loved the show. I enjoy it. Just about everybody does who's a fan of old-time radio. Sure, it's corny sometimes and overblown, but it's what made radio great—it fed the imagination.

"Thus endeth the lesson," Tucker joked.

"So the original run is what collectors want to find?" Courtney asked. She gestured to the window. "Do you mind?"

"No, go ahead."

She rolled the window down to let the wind blow through her hair. "And the value is merely fan driven then?"

"To answer your first question, any disc at this point is important, but yeah, the Hollywood run is the 'holy grail' that Bobby went on about. And yes, the fans are the ones who are mainly interested because the show is lost to the passage of time. It's not new and hip, or whatever."

"Worth any money?"

"That's debatable since no complete serials of the run have been found. But because it's reached mythical proportions, I'm sure whoever found them, if there are any to be found, could charge what he wanted," Tucker said. He slowed down to exit off the highway toward Puskatahaw. "Most fans just want the shows found so they can hear them. That's all they want."

"One of them doesn't."

"If I'm right about this. Who knows? This could be a long-lost G.I. Joe nurse figure that goes up in price every year."

"I'm so amazed that you know all this, Tucker."

"Thanks to Bobby. I was just a fan, but he educated me."

"What if it's a disc?" she asked.

He hadn't gotten past getting into the post office box. "I don't know."

"What would Bobby want?"

"I'm not a hundred percent of that, either."

"Well, he did set it up for you to find. He's leaving it up to you."

"I know. And that scares me a little." Images of Bobby bleeding out his life all alone flashed in his mind.

"Give the key to Stiles and let him do it then, if it bothers you," she suggested.

"No. He sent it to me. He's asking me to take care of it."

"What about whoever's out there?"

"I'm trying not to think about that."

"Bobby's Nebraska connection, you think?" she asked sparked by curiosity.

"I just want to get to the post office and go from there, Courtney."

"Gotcha." She became silent.

"I'm a bear to deal with, huh?" he asked.

"It's understandable. I'm sure I'd be pulling my hair out at this point. One question just leads to another."

"I know. One thing at a time."

He swung onto the deserted main street of Puskatahaw. A close neighbor to Lyle, it had its economic base in ag and oil like most towns in the area. The town hadn't grown as fast or as big as Lyle, but it possessed a charm all its own. Tucker passed the Full Tank Gas Station and turned down a side street.

"Their little post office isn't on Main Street," he commented.

"Unlike every other town in Oklahoma, huh?" Courtney chimed in.

He parked in front, but didn't see Stiles. Without waiting for him, he hopped out of the car and into the lobby of the post office. The air conditioning hit him full in the face as he walked in. He shivered, not so much from the A/C, but from anticipation. He sensed Bobby's presence here. This is just like Bobby, he thought, using a post office box in a nearby town to keep his actions secret.

"Which one is it?" Courtney asked. She ran a finger down the scroll work on the front of the post office boxes that hailed back to the forties. "What's on the key?"

"Seventy-five A," Tucker said finding the correct box down low. Needing to be big to accommodate the sixteen inch transcription discs, the box had been built down close to the floor where larger items could be handled more easily. The smaller boxes for mail and handheld packages were higher up.

Tucker knelt down in the front of the box with the key in his hand. He heard a car pull up in the parking lot outside.

"Is that Stiles?" he asked.

"It's not a car I recognize."

Tucker jumped to his feet just as Stiles got out of his vehicles.

"I nearly had a heart attack for a second," Tucker confessed. "I could just see…" He didn't finish the sentence. He refused to imagine violence happening to either one of them. He pushed it out of his mind.

"Open it up," Courtney said.

Tucker slid the key in the lock and turned. The metal door opened easily. He pulled out a square cardboard package that had tape wrapped around it multiple times.

"What'd I miss?" Stiles asked as he shoved the door against the wall. He sprang over to see Tucker open the package.

Tucker pulled a pocketknife out and cut the layers of tape. Anticipating as much as he was, Stiles and

Courtney helped pull the tape off the cardboard. Courtney wadded up a ball of it and flung it to the floor.

"Man, did he ever pack that good," Stiles observed.

"It'll be stuffed with bubble wrap, too. He paid the most to have it shipped without it getting banged around. That would have broken the disc," Tucker explained.

He removed the last of the tape, sliced the edge of the box, and carefully peeled back the cardboard. Just as he predicted, bubble wrap filled the box to the brim.

"Use this," Stiles commanded him as he gave him a handkerchief.

"What for?"

"We can get fingerprints off the paper."

"Right."

Gripping as much of it as he could, he pulled the bubble wrap and what lay inside it out of the box. He handed the box to Stiles who studied it for any kind of clue.

"It looks like a record," Courtney said.

"A big one," Stiles commented.

"The discs were sixteen inches, most of them, anyway," Tucker clarified.

He sliced the tape holding the bubble wrap in place. Slowly unraveling the wrap, Tucker removed a transcription disc protected in a paper sleeve. He dropped the wrapping and placed the disc on a counter near the front window. His jaw nearly fell a mile.

"He found one," he whispered. "You found one," he said as if Bobby stood beside him.

"Is it what you thought?" Courtney asked. She tiptoed to look over his shoulder for a peek.

"According to the label, it's an episode from July of '39," Tucker reported. He closed his eyes trying to recall what he knew of the show's history. "That would make it the first season, but the label doesn't have a serial title. I'm not sure which one this is."

"Does it matter?" Stiles asked.

"To a collector it does. As far as I know, this is the only disc of this episode in existence."

"Making it valuable then," Stiles remarked.

"I'm not sure in dollar amount. I don't have any idea. But to a collector, this was worth killing for."

"That's right," Stiles said reaching for the disc.

"What are you doing?" Tucker asked.

"Now it's evidence. I'll need to run this for prints on the sleeve, the label, and the disc and then it gets boxed up," Stiles explained.

Tucker fought the instinctive urge to run out of the post office with his friend's discovery clutched to his chest. Courtney saw his consternation and touched him on the arm.

"This is a piece of the past, Stiles. I have to get it on the air tonight. I have to," Tucker nearly yelled. "And don't stand there and give me all the rules and regulations about how to conduct a murder investigation. This was my friend we're talking about here. He died for this. The only way to honor him is to play it on tonight's show, which means I have to take it to his house and use his player to record it so I can use in on the air."

"I appreciate you finding this, Tucker. I really do. But as you said, there are rules and regulations. It's called the law. I can't allow this to be tampered with anymore than it already has been. I'm going to have to take the packaging, the bubble wrap, and everything else and have them fingerprinted and analyzed."

"I'm playing this show tonight, Stiles. That is final. This is my property now," Tucker said, his panic starting to paralyze him.

"It's your property and I understand that. But right now it's a piece of evidence in a murder case. I'm going to have to call Detective Phelps in Lincoln; I have to log it into the evidence locker, and see where it leads us."

"I don't care if you need to deliver it to the Library of Congress," Tucker challenged. "I am playing this on the air."

"How long will it take to fingerprint it, Detective?" Courtney asked, breaking the tension between the two men.

"A couple of hours at least."

"Tucker," she continued, "how long to cut a recording?"

"An hour or so, I have to set up his player and set up a recorder," Tucker mumbled.

"If you're there to supervise, would this be okay after you fingerprint it, Detective?"

Stiles shrugged his shoulders, but conceded: "I'll ask the tech, but that could probably work." He looked directly at Tucker. "But then it goes back to the station in the evidence locker. If we get whoever did this, it'll have to be submitted at the trial."

"Tucker, can you deal with that?" Courtney asked, still touching his arm.

"It doesn't matter if he can deal with it, ma'am, it's a matter of the law," Stiles reminded her. She acted like she didn't hear him.

"Tucker?"

"Of course. I'm being an idiot about it, I know. I just want to air it tonight. I want to share it with everybody out there. I'm going to send word out on the Llama's website and to every radio fan I'm in contact with. If this is Bobby's legacy, I'm going to get it out there. It's the least, the very least, I can do for him. I don't know any other way of doing it…"

"You've forgotten something, Tucker," Stiles interrupted.

"What now?"

"You'll be letting the murderer know as well. Have you thought about that?"

"Not until you just said it."

"That change your mind?"

Tucker didn't hesitate: "Not one bit."

"Keep me on speed dial then."

"Okay."

"Got it," Stiles pressed.

"I got it."

Chapter Seventeen

"You bet, honey, Bellevue boasted big time about having hundreds of the *I Love a Mystery* shows in his collection," Julia Appleton agreed. Tucker caught her at home with his second Skype request, this time from his house, instead of the station. "As far as I know, there isn't a way to tell that if he didn't put anything on the sleeve, label, or the disc itself."

"Not as far as I know," Tucker said.

"And you're playing it tonight?"

"If I get it back in time from the police."

"You need to know that our Tony Boucher sent in a lot of letters to the fanzines back in the day bragging about swiping shows from Bellevue."

"You said that before."

"I'm talking about *I Love a Mystery*."

"He bragged about stealing *I Love a Mystery*?" Tucker asked, nervous again. "A few fragments, or what?"

"He said entire runs, but who knows? The man was a liar and I'm not sure if anyone out there knew who he was. Ego-maniacs have big mouths, but like to keep in the shadows at the same time."

"It doesn't take a genius to figure what two and two equals here."

"No, it doesn't, honey," Julia agreed. "If your disc is what you say it is, nobody's heard that since the original run by in '39. Well, of course, Bellevue probably, and our mysterious Boucher."

"Bobby found Boucher then. That's the only explanation I've got."

"The police do know about this, you say?" she asked, getting nervous herself.

"They do. But they don't understand it any better than I do and I've told them everything I know."

"That's a good thing."

"Thank you, Julia."

"No, thank you. You've given this old lady another great topic for an article that only four people will read. I can't wait to get started," she commented, not hiding the sarcasm.

"Make it five."

"That better be a promise. Bye now."

The Skype session ended.

Tucker turned his attention to updating the Llama's website with quick, catchy blurbs on the news page and *The Golden Age of Yesteryear*'s link. He zipped off a program change note to all the subscribers to the show's newsletter. And finally, he recorded two spots with similar verbiage, but with a different music bed and uploaded them into the computer system. He set them to play in fifteen minute intervals, flip-flopping from one to the other with each commercial break.

With the sun nearly down, he rang up Stiles who said he would gladly meet him at Bobby's house with the disc, which he would transport back to the police station after Tucker finished.

Checking for his car keys, Tucker decided to do what he knew to be the most idiotic thing he could. He dialed Dave Geiser with the news knowing full well that Dave acted as the clique's town crier. Within a matter of minutes, everyone in Lincoln connected to Bobby would know about the fragment episode.

He wanted to call Courtney for a late supper, but quickly retreated back into the hole inside himself he'd been so careful to dig. She pegged him every time they talked. He didn't like it, but he accepted it. Too much emotion tore at him—Bobby's demise, the loss of his wife, the disc, and everything else in his lousy life pulled him in all directions. He would see her later tonight at the broadcast.

At the back door, he nearly ran over Jackson Mulroy. They did a sideways dance and Tucker let him pass.

"Hey Tucker, got your show ready for tonight?" Jackson asked politely.

"I think I do, yeah."

"What is it? That old radio stuff? I guess it does well 'cos Hibler keeps buying spots from us and putting money in the coffers."

Tucker detected a hint of Jackson playing dumb. But only just a hint.

"Yeah, I'm dedicating tonight's show to my friend who was killed...murdered. I thought it would be a nice send off."

Jackson scratched absently at a spot on his temple. "That stinks, Tucker. Not about the show and your...dedication thing, but that he was killed. Bobby Ross, right?"

"Yes."

"He was a collector or something?" Jackson asked.

"A little more than that, but, yes, he collected."

"I'm sorry about your loss." Jackson patted him on the shoulder more than necessary. "I heard the spot for it coming in. A 'long lost' episode of some show? What's that about?"

"Just that. A show from a program that was thought to be lost."

"But now is found," Jackson commented making a wry reference to the parable of the lost son in the Bible.

"Something like that."

"Well, I need to look over a couple of accounts before tomorrow morning," Jackson explained, which he rarely did for Tucker, or anyone at the station. "I have breakfast at Rotary in the morning and the manager for the Ford place will be there. I want to get some numbers right."

"Have fun with that, Jackson."

"I'll try to. Have a good show, Tucker."

Jackson disappeared behind the closed door, leaving Tucker there wondering what the whole conversation had been about. Paranoid now at every nuance, Tucker shrugged it off, got into his car, and took off for Bobby's.

Stiles sat on the front porch holding an extra large plastic bag, which held the ET in it. Tucker mumbled a hello and took the disc from him. Stiles lumbered into the house behind him.

"I sure hope your techies used gloves on this baby," Tucker said.

"Of course they do. I told you they do, Tucker. Man, you're breaking my back over this. You're lucky I could even bring to you. Thankfully, the chief is off on Sundays."

Tucker took a pair of soft cotton gloves Bobby kept in a desk drawer in his disc room. He prepared the special player and set the disc onto it.

"I have a record player at my house, you know," Stiles said.

"Bite your tongue. A regular LP record player won't do you any good with these babies." He grabbed his laptop from his satchel and set it up on the desk.

Stiles pulled his jacket collar close to his neck. "I didn't mention before, but this room is a tad on the coolish side."

"Has to be to store these. They're still deteriorating, but that's life. Everything erodes into nothing after a while."

"Your philosophy of life can bring a guy down, Tucker."

"I don't have time to fiddle around here."

"Hey, since when do those old players hook up with your computer?" Stiles asked.

"Bobby had it done so he could eliminate all the steps to get the shows in a digitized format. Most shows were recorded from the transcription discs to reel-to-reel and then from reel-to-reel to cassette and then to another cassette and so forth and so on until collectors were ending up with shows that were four times, or more, removed from the original master recording of the show."

"This cuts out all the middle man steps, so to speak," Stiles joked.

"Yes, it does and it saves on ever playing this disc again."

"You're kidding me, right? You won't ever play that disc again?"

"Not after I get it on my computer, I won't. Why?"

"Man, that is crazy."

"What is?"

"This whole hobby. So you search like crazy to find all these old records."

"Transcription discs, or ETs, or even platters, but don't call them records, Stiles," Tucker corrected.

"So you get these *ETs* and you record them and then you stack them up in these knothead shelves so you can take them out every once in a while and look at them. Are you absolutely kidding me?"

"You don't understand collecting."

"From my end of it, it looks like a different brand of nuts."

Tucker bit back a retort so he could focus on opening up a folder labeled "ILAM." He opened his recording software on his laptop and set a level. Bobby had recruited him to do this before, so he knew the input by heart.

"Not to say your friend was nuts, Tucker," Stiles said. "I'm a cynic from the top of my head down to my boots. To me, enjoying something for its aesthetic value is just a way of someone trying to be arrogant."

"In some cases I would agree."

"But Bobby wasn't that way?"

"Not all the time."

"I wish I could get it."

"Are you a sports lover?" Tucker asked. "You like football, basketball?"

"Sooner football, crimson and cream."

"That doesn't make any sense to me. See?"

"Yeah, but who said there's any aesthetic value in a football game?" Stiles joked. Tucker actually laughed. "You're not happy with me."

"No, I'm not."

"Last week when you thought I accused you…"

"You did accuse me. I thought you genuine. You lured me in so you could get information."

"Only a little. I'd like to think I'm genuine, even if I am a detective and see the underbelly of life every day."

Tucker started the file recording, lifted the arm on the player, and set it on the disc. Scratchy pops and blips reverberated through the speaker on the machine. Tucker held up a hand. He wanted to listen.

In the span of fifteen minutes, Tucker transported back to another time when innocence abounded and entertainment reflected it. The actors' voices blended so well together. Michael Raffetto's deep baritone brought the character of Jack Packard to life. Barton

Yarborough played Doc Long, the lanky Texan who made proclamations with a devil-may-care attitude. Finishing out the adventurous trio, Walter Paterson, once of the British stage, portrayed Reggie York, the bruiser of the group.

Later, Tucker couldn't recall much of the story of the episode. He melted away into the experience of it all. The thought came to him that he was the first person in ages who had heard this. Why would anyone horde these away and not share them with the rest of the world? It was inconceivable. He imagined himself as an eleven-year-old kid hiding under the covers late at night listening to this on a Philco radio with the dial glowing warmly in the mystery-filled night.

The show ended abruptly. He shut the machine down, stopped the recording on his laptop, and sat quietly in front of the stack of transcription discs. Stiles knew well enough to leave him alone. He exited the room and back out onto the front porch to wait.

Maybe not the best episode of the series, Tucker thought, but in a matter of hours he would be playing it back on the air for the first time in over seventy years. Not a boaster by nature, he silently chalked it up as a win—for himself and for Bobby.

Suddenly feeling brave, he took out his phone, snapped a pic of the label core of the disc, and uploaded it to the *Yesteryear* page he had created on Facebook a few months back. If the trio from *I Love a Mystery* were around today, he thought, it would have been something they would have done. He didn't like the melodramatic phrase "flushing out a killer," but it would have to do.

Tucker had put as much bait out there as he could manage. He knew he should tell Stiles, but couldn't. He didn't have a solid, logical reason. He didn't need one.

He shut the equipment down and locked up. Stiles took the disc from him and sealed it back in the plastic bag.

"Have a good show," Stiles said.

"I hope to. I really do."

Chapter Eighteen

Back at the radio station, Tucker checked his e-mail and the message board for *Yesteryear*. The counter number was higher and his inbox had a few new e-mails all requesting more info about the missing episode. Knowing full well the networking of the hobby, Tucker banked that anyone who held interest in *I Love a Mystery* would be tuning into the show tonight. He also knew that any speculation or rumor would fuel the curiosity.

The identity of a few of the e-mail senders was cleverly masked with odd ID names, but all threatened. From the absurd to the ludicrous, many of these e-mails ranted about flooding the airwaves with something sacred to claiming ownership of the missing show. Nearly deleting them, he put them into a special folder in case Stiles needed them later.

The mood from most of the e-mails was positive. The true fans panted for a new episode. Computers were ready to record the online version of the program. Tucker knew that in a matter of hours this fragment from the series would be available from many of the traders out there. Sadly, he also knew that there would be a fee charged by some of the less scrupulous dealers, who used the hobby as a way to supplement their income.

But he couldn't do anything about that. Nor, did he care to.

"Knock-knock," Courtney said from the door nearly causing him to jump out of his chair. "Sorry about that. I didn't mean to scare you."

"You didn't. I scared myself. What are you doing here?"

"I asked you if I could sit in with you on the show tonight."

He snapped his fingers. "That's right. Duh! I'm a goof. I've been a million miles away since the post office," he said.

She held up a bag from *The Feedbag*, a cleverly named eatery that opened on Sunday afternoons and catered to the evening church crowds. Courtney put the bag on his desk and handed him a soda.

"I only guessed, mind you, but I thought you looked like a chicken breast on whole wheat with mayo and pickles, but hold the onions."

"I look like that?" he tried to joke, but failed miserably.

"And tots."

"You should win a prize. Thank you. You didn't have to get me any supper," he said while he tore into the bag and spread the contents on his desk.

"I guessed you wouldn't have eaten."

"Another good guess."

"I *guess* so."

He laughed at the good natured quip all the while searching for a knife to carve his sandwich in half. Courtney held one out to him. He quietly thanked her and set to the task of eating.

"I want to say something to you," he said through a mouthful of tater tots.

"Okay," she answered with some trepidation.

"I want to apologize."

"What for?"

"For being what I am. For not knowing what to say to you half the time and for ignoring you the other. I don't know why you're interested in being my friend, but I appreciate it. I'm scared of it, but I appreciate it." Before he could stop it, tears rolled down the sides of his face. "And because I miss my wife so much."

He put the sandwich down on the desk and his head in his hands. Courtney didn't move from her spot across from him. She knew better than ease the grief pouring out. He needed this more than anything else in the world. No wailing echoed through the hallway. He didn't beat his fists against the desk. He didn't blubber about the unfairness of the uncaring, cold universe.

He just let it all out. For so long he corked the anger, guilt, confusion, loss, and rage. He imagined shoving all the memories and feelings that tore at his heart into a deep bottle buried in a dark place with him shoving the cork in the neck to keep it all from escaping. Now he couldn't put it all back if he tried.

Courtney set her sandwich down and left the room. She'd been there a few months back when her aunt had passed. She remembered the day she lost it. It embarrassed her, but the release of it took a weight off of her. Tucker needed it. She would get out of his office and let him have it.

She checked the front door to make sure it was locked and other busy work to keep her away from Tucker's office. She waved at Mose who came in from the back entrance.

"Hi there, Mose. Weren't you in earlier today?"

"Yes, I was, but Mr. Mulroy called the answering service saying something about the men's room needing to be checked out."

"You didn't have to come back for that, Mose. Jackson isn't even here on the weekends."

"He was today. Excuse me."

"I'm sure it could wait 'til tomorrow."

"Not if it's that pesky toilet again."

"You're not the plumber, Mose. Don't let Jackson push you around."

Mose turned and smiled a toothy grin at her. "Don't you worry about that. But if that toilet is being persnickety, it makes my cleaning crew grumpy and that's a bad thing."

She rolled her eyes playfully at him. Mose disappeared into the men's room. Courtney could hear him muttering to the toilet about not living the right kind of life. She checked her watch. Tucker had fifteen minutes before air time.

Walking in like nothing happened, Courtney plopped down into the chair across from the desk. She checked her grilled ham and cheese and was pleasantly surprised to find it still warm.

"Your sandwich got cold," Tucker said without a word about his meltdown. "I zapped it in the microwave for you."

"Thanks, Tucker." She bit into it.

"I'm going on into the control room. You wanna come in there or wait until I start the show?"

She grabbed her food and soda. "I'll tag along now if that's all right."

"Let me show you how a pro sits in the saddle," he said with a wink. "You might want to take some notes."

"I'll do that."

Courtney grabbed the stool on the other side of the counter where they conducted interviews with local business owners or school teachers, or other interesting citizens of Lyle. She spread her food out and observed Tucker's routine behind the board.

Each DJ did their own thing to prep for the show. Some tapped the mic off air with headphones on to see if it worked, others spun in the chair, and she'd seen a

DJ or two shuck down to boxer shorts for their time slot.

Tucker fanned out pieces of paper with notes in front of him. He made a notation here and there. Checking the computer system, he verified, yet again, that the missing show had uploaded okay. Finally, he slid the headphones around his neck and hummed a lonely tune.

Not the most exciting set up she'd ever seen, but definitely his own. She finished up her meal, dumped the bag into the waste basket, and plopped back down in the chair. They had five minutes to go.

"You nervous?" she asked.

Tucker held up a quivering hand. "Not at all," he quipped.

"You're going to do fine."

"Is there something you want to tell me?"

She shot him a quizzical look. "Like what?"

"I just thought you might have something you wanted to say before I started the show."

"I can't think of a thing. I want to see the master at work."

"It's the lamest question in the world, but why?"

"Why? You're right, that is pretty lame. Does there have to be a reason right now this very minute?"

"It would ease my mind."

"I doubt that. You're wound up pretty tight."

"Like a 'nine day clock' my dad would've said."

She laughed. "That's a good description."

"I'm not sure what you want from me."

"Who said I wanted anything?"

"The timing is either really awful, or really coincidental."

She frowned at him. "Your questions only get you more questions. I'm just a gal wanting to sit and watch you do the show."

"That's not what I'm talking about and you know it," he said.

"I know what you're referring to, but I'm in the mood for some old radio."

"That's old-*time* radio," he corrected.

"See? I'm learning things already. I'm sure you'll have all kinds of nuggets to tell your listeners."

"You're good at dodging the issue."

"There isn't any issue from where I'm sitting, Tucker. You're just nervous and tense and you want to do this for Bobby. Just relax. It's all going to be fine."

"There you are being right again. That's an annoying habit you have."

"He would approve, Tucker. You know he would."

"Maybe so. Sometimes you never knew with Bobby."

She pointed at the clock. He whipped around and put his hand on the control board.

"You're on in ten," she said. "Knock 'em dead."

"I wish you wouldn't say it like that," he managed to say before the hour struck. He pushed the slider up, opening the mic and started his chatter prepping tonight's audience for a special evening of old-time radio, a dedication to a friend, and the premiere of a missing *I Love a Mystery* episode.

"But to whet your appetites for that, we're going to start off with a favorite episode of my friend Bobby Ross. Okay, so for the aficionado it's an old standby and we all know it, but for the newcomer to old-time radio it's a classic. That's right, gang, one and all, dredgers of the night, it's *The Hitchhiker*, and I thought we would listen to the 1942 *Suspense* version. Strap yourselves in harbingers of the airwaves, this is a good one."

Tucker brought the mic out, punched the computer with the file for the show on dock, and brought the first dark chimes of the show. The announcer proclaimed that the show was brought to the public by the Columbia Network. Tucker balanced the output and set his headphones down on the counter in front of the control panel.

Courtney closed her eyes as Orson Welles led the show off with a wordy introduction. His deep, timbered voice announced that the script was a classic of the medium. Courtney absorbed his hypnotic vocal patterns. She envisioned the young Welles with shirt sleeves rolled up to his elbows reading the words from the page. She understood Tucker's fascination with the hobby. This type of radio had the aura of power behind it.

"Captivated already?" Tucker asked. "It's like that, isn't it? I feel it every time I play a show no matter how good or bad it is. I wish I'd been around in those days to hear these shows for the first time."

"You think you would have recognized its charm then?"

"Absolutely. No question about it."

"Do you mind if I use the headphones?" she asked already leaning over to get them.

"Go right ahead." He handed them to her. She pulled the cuffs over her ears just as the transition music played and Welles started his narration of the story. She sat back in her chair shutting her eyes again so the "theatre of the mind" could take over.

Tucker, having heard the shows dozens of times, snuck out of the booth to steal a few quick minutes to suck down some nicotine. Mose met him in the hallway.

"Mose, you stay here anymore and we'll have to name a wing after you," he kidded.

"That lousy toilet again is making my life miserable."

"I'll have somebody call a plumber tomorrow."

"You do that," Mose said not hiding his consternation. "I'm going for a smoke. I assume that's where you're headed?"

"Yes, sir. Last one there…"

"Yeah, yeah. Cut the dialogue. I wanna smoke," Mose said opening the back door.

Down the hall, Courtney waved at Tucker to get his attention. She frantically hissed: "You've got a caller!"

"Oh, great," Tucker moaned. He rarely ever got phone calls. He could bet a dollar as to what the caller wanted.

"Taking a rain check, Mose. Have fun."

"You know it. Talk to you later, Tucker," Mose said as the door shut softly behind him.

Tucker hopped back into the saddle in the control booth and grabbed the phone from Courtney's hand. Before he could give a greeting, the caller on the other end demanded to know when the missing *I Love a Mystery* episode would air. Tucker interrupted unsuccessfully to let the caller know it would be the last show of the night, but the guy on the other end, obviously a rabid fan, would hear none of it.

Tucker covered the phone with the palm of his hand. "I think I need to hang up on the guy. He's going on and on."

"We get those."

The caller ranted for another minute when Tucker plunged into the conversation informing him that he would need to be patient and wait. He used the "saving the best for last" cliché before saying goodbye.

"I haven't had a caller in three weeks for this show," he said. "Now they decide to call."

As if on cue, the phone rang again. He checked the time. The *Suspense* episode had another twenty minutes or so left. He grabbed the phone and sat through another tirade of yet another fan of the beloved show by Carlton E. Morse. This time he had a pat answer ready, shot it out, and said a perfunctory goodbye.

"This is getting easier." The phone rang again. "I think."

"You might want to check your e-mail, too," Courtney suggested.

"Cover that for me," he said without thinking. As he reached for the phone, he caught himself. "I'm sorry. Where did that come from? Would you please? Or, don't if you don't want to. Here I am snapping my fingers like I was somebody."

"Or, Jackson," she said. "Sure. You want me to use the computer here..?"

"Why not use the one in my office? If there are any that are pressing, let me know and I'll do something about it. Maybe I should play missing shows more often. This is wild," he said. He finally answered the call on the fourth ring.

"KLMA, the Llama, how are you, sir?" He covered the phone again. "My e-mail is already opened up."

Courtney nodded and left him to it. She flopped in his chair, found his inbox, and popped it open with a click of the mouse. Sure enough, over a dozen e-mails flooded his inbox with similar phrases in the subject line wanting to know more about the missing *I Love a Mystery* episode. She scanned through them from top to bottom before clicking open the most recent e-mail.

In a matter of minutes she realized that there were a lot of fans who claimed personal ownership of the ancient radio program. She read the self-proclamations boasting being "an important fan" of the forgotten adventure show. She printed off the most accessible for Tucker to answer. There were a few that she was sure he wouldn't respond to as the level of rabid appreciation for the program bordered on the certifiable.

One user name caught her attention. She sent it to the printer immediately and went back to reading through the rest.

Absorbed completely in a world she knew little about, she lost track of time. She stretched her back out seeing the clock on the wall. She missed the change over from *Suspense* to a show she didn't recognize. She strained to hear through the speaker hanging on Tucker's wall, but couldn't make out much. Grabbing the stack of printed e-mails, Courtney noticed the order of shows scribbled on Tucker's desk. *Fred Allen* was next in the lineup.

She also noticed the smoke pouring in through the vents.

"Tucker, we've got to get out of here," she gasped turning the corner into the control booth.

"Goodbye, sir. Be patient," he said into the phone. "What do you mean we need to get out of here? If I leave here, the phone lines will fry."

"If we stay in here, we'll fry as well."

She pointed to the overheard vent that just began streaming in a thin wispy arm of smoke into the booth. He jerked to his feet. Finding his cell phone in his back pocket, he hustled to the front door with Courtney right behind him.

Just as he reached for the handle, he stopped himself.

"Tucker, let's get out of here. Call 9-1-1!" Courtney screeched.

"Hold on! Get away from the door!" He grabbed her by the arm jerking her back toward the control booth. He stood in the middle of the smoke and started coughing viciously.

"The building in on fire, Tucker! We need to get out of here! Forget your show!" she yelled at him. "It's not worth it!"

His eyes were streaming tears all over his face. "It's not a fire!"

"Where there's smoke, Tucker!"

"Not this time. I flushed out a killer! Take a whiff. Not a big one, but do it."

"Tucker."

"Just do it. We may not have a whole lotta time here."

She stuck her head in the smoke and took a short breath. She instantly gagged and tears sprang into her eyes.

"Does that smell like smoke from a fire to you?"

"You could've told me it was tear gas! I would've believed you! This stuff can make you go blind if you're not careful," she complained.

"Sorry, you're right. I'm not thinking here!" He dialed Stiles' direct number. It rang a couple of times before he answered.

"Hey Tucker, I thought you were doing a radio show?" he said.

"Get over the station right now!" Tucker moved close to the lobby and peeked around the corner. He peered through the glass front that framed the outer door. He couldn't see anything out in the front parking lot.

"Tucker!" Stiles yelled.

"Bring everybody on duty, Stiles."

"What is going on?"

Tucker thought he saw movement in the shadows near the street lamp. Courtney edged around the corner with him to see if she could see anything. The tears streamed down both their faces.

"Tucker, you need to tell me what is going on," Stiles said trying to take control of the situation.

"Get over here now!" Movement near the lamp caught his attention. "Just do it!" He hung up the phone and stuck his head back into the control room. The program played, no problem, and all the other shows were in the cue on the computer. Not that having dead air would be the end of the world compared to getting killed, but he needed to have that lost show play.

Tear gas still filled the room with a hazy fog.

"Tucker, we need to get out of this building," Courtney said. "We aren't safe in here."

"Whoever is doing this is trying to get us to go outside. We can't. We're dead if we go out there. We just need to stay put and wait for Stiles to get here."

"But this whole place is filling with tear gas," she said gasping for breath. She coughed hard and moved toward the hallway. White gas hung in the air of the hallway gently sinking toward the floor. "There is no way we can stay in here, Tucker. We have got to get out of here!" Her desperation pulled her toward the lobby to see if anyone lurked there.

Tucker grabbed her and pulled her back. "Just a minute or two more, Courtney." He gagged on the smoke and coughed until his lungs ached. A sudden thought hit him: "Wasn't Mose just here? He went out the back for a smoke."

Before she could answer, a loud pop echoed from the front parking lot. A half second behind it, the glass exploded into the lobby of the station. Tucker caught a glimpse of someone holding a pistol standing under the light of the street lamp.

"The back! Go, go, go!" he yelled dragging Courtney after him.

"I don't have the keys to my car!" she wailed.

"I do! Come on, come on, come on!"

As he put his hand on the door, he halted. She ran into him and reached around to shove the door open.

"Wait!" he yelled. He couldn't see anyone pursuing them down the hallway. The killer knew they would hightail it to the back door and make a run for it. "He's still trying to get us out of the building. He's not sure of the layout, so he's getting us out in the open."

"Tucker, this tear gas is about to rip my lungs out," she said. The tears poured from her eyes ruining her mascara. She looked like a raccoon with black caked on top of her cheek bones.

"Where are they?" Tucker asked. His fury couldn't be held back now. Never had anyone tried to kill him. The trap frightened him and what made it worse was Courtney being caught with him.

He thought he heard his name yelled from outside the door.

"What was that?" Courtney asked. "Is that..?"

"I'm not sure." He ran back down the hall and told her to wait. It didn't occur to him before, but with the tear gas coming through the duct work, that meant the fan from the air conditioner circulated it into the station.

Tucker shut the A/C off on the thermostat. The fans shut off leaving the gas to hang heavy in the air. Tucker waved his arms through it as he returned to the rear of the station.

"I wish I'd have thought of that," Courtney said. "All we had to do was shut off the A/C. I feel like an idiot."

"I don't think it matters. He would've found a way. Somehow."

Outside the door, they heard footsteps thump against the concrete only a few feet away. Instinctually, Courtney backed away and pointed.

She mouthed: "He's coming through the back door."

Tucker held up a hand to calm her down.

The door handle turned slowly, but stopped. The lock held it fast. The handle turned the other direction. It wouldn't budge. A fist hit against the wall. Tucker moved to Courtney without making a sound.

Whoever it was jerked hard on the door trying to rip it open. The lock held it fast. Just as quickly as it started, it quit. Tucker strained to hear anything from the other side. He thought he heard someone speaking, but he couldn't make out any words. A metallic click came from the other side of the door.

Without saying a thing, Tucker wrapped his arms tight around Courtney and dove for the floor. The air shoved out of her lungs and she thought she felt a rib pop out of place. He covered her body with his own just as two shots ripped through the metal covering on the door.

Tucker froze. He didn't know what else to do. If they got back up and ran out the front, they would be visible. If they stayed, the killer could somehow get the back door opened. The absurdity of the trap nearly made him laugh. And to make it worse, the tear gas sank down the floor level.

Courtney remained still pinned underneath him not daring to make a sound. Another shot hit the door, this time the lock. She heard the remains of it pop out with bits of steel spraying the floor.

"He shot the lock, Tucker," she whispered.

He sprang to his knees, grabbed her hands, and pulled her to her feet just as another shot slammed into the door with another sound crying off into the distance.

"They made it. Finally!"

The sirens screamed outside with their flashers blazing blue and red in front of the radio station. Another cruiser whipped around to the rear of the building. The sounds of doors opening, radios squawking, and police calling out filled the air.

Tucker thought it the sweetest thing he'd heard in a long time.

An officer called out from the lobby. Tucker answered back. They stayed put. A knock tapped at the back door nearly sending them to the floor again.

"Tucker?" Stiles yelled from the other side. "You in there?"

"Yes. Can we come out?"

"Is anyone in there with you?" Stiles asked with a sense of urgency.

"Courtney Cannon. Nobody else."

There was a pause. Tucker could hear Stiles talking into a two-way radio confirming with the officer in the lobby that they were, in fact, alone.

"Okay, come on out," Stiles ordered.

Tucker pushed the door open, allowing Courtney and him to fill their lungs with much needed air. He watched as Courtney leaned over a car hacking the gas out of her lungs.

"We're okay, we're okay," Tucker repeated over and over. "No one was hurt."

Stiles motioned to an officer checking the pulse of someone on the pavement. "Except for him."

Tucker stepped forward and saw Mose with blood streaming down his forehead. He bent over double, coughing until he threw up on the ground.

Chapter Nineteen

The dream came this time more vivid, detailed than it ever had been. In this version the faces were clearer, sharper somehow. Voices were discernible and he heard the soft lilt in every word she spoke. Her face beamed. She didn't hold a grudge against him for not going. The rain dripped off the edge of the roof where he promised a gutter would be one day. An occasional flash of lightning touched a crooked finger toward the earth.

Images tangled themselves into other pictures. Smoke filled the landscape. The horizon burned a deep hue of buttery yellow. Departed family members and friends fanned out quickly then faded from view. Their old car sailed through on a road already soaked. The curve loomed in the distance.

He watched. The inevitable happened again.

A fuzzy bright beam of light glared under his upturned eyelid. He tried to force it shut, but failed. The same thing happened to the other eyelid. A small trickle of a tear pushed down his cheek. Voices sounding like they existed under water grumbled strange words at him.

"Did the show play on the air?" he managed to ask. His tongue had grown fur since the last he'd checked. He ran it over his teeth. Every sensation burned anew. Blinking, he finally became conscious of where he was.

"It played," a stranger's voice answered him.

"It played what?" he croaked. What was this guy talking about, anyway?

"Wakey, wakey, Tucker," the voice commanded. He didn't like the voice.

With a jerk of his head, he popped forward. Fully alert, he recognized Adam Stiles, Denise, and Rhonda standing around his hospital bed.

"Is Courtney all right? What about Mose? Did you find the guy who tried to kill us? What's going?" he rattled off in one quick breath.

"Whoa, one at a time," Stiles said.

"Courtney is fine. Is that her name?" Denise said.

"She works with me at the station."

"You both had a shock and you breathed in a lot of tear gas," Stiles explained.

"Mose is going to be all right, too, but it'll take a little bit longer," Denise said. "I've been sitting with him and his family half the night. We go back a ways."

"Our perp busted him on the head when he wouldn't give him his keys to the back door," Stiles said. "We found the keys on the other side of the parking lot under a clump of bushes. My guess is that Mose threw them there when he figured out that this guy was going to hurt you."

"Did he get a look at him?" Tucker asked.

"He's in and out. He took a hard hit on his head. What I can get out of him doesn't make any sense. We're waiting."

Tucker realized that Rhonda stood at the foot of his bed. His face flushed with anger.

"Ask her!"

"Tucker," she began, but he cut her off.

"It was her! Stiles! It was her! She's one of Bobby's contacts from Lincoln," he yelled. He didn't care if he was in a hospital bed.

Stiles pushed him back onto the bed ever-so gently. "Take a chill pill, Tucker. She got in last night. And before you ask, we verified her flight's arrival time in Oklahoma City."

"I stayed in a hotel last night," she said. "Who would do this to you?"

"I thought you would," Tucker said unashamed. "I thought you couldn't afford to come down here?"

"Dave loaned me the money. He wanted to come, too, but he couldn't get out of work. Lee and Jacob flew in on Saturday and drove up to Tulsa to see some friends."

"They flew in on Saturday?" Tucker asked. His fear rose up in him again. "How do we know they went to Tulsa?"

"I'm working on it," Stiles said doing his best to keep him calm.

"What about Randy? Was he coming as well?"

"He had to keep Trader Book's open as long as he could, he said," Rhonda told him. "He still wasn't a hundred percent sure he would even make it."

Stiles patted Tucker's shoulder. "Don't go accusing everybody you can think of. The police are doing everything they can right now. We have a few more pieces of evidence to follow."

"Was there any footage from the cameras in the parking lot?" Tucker asked.

"Those things are only for show and have been for a while now. But we do have shell casings, which can tell us something about the gun."

"Yeah, it goes *boom*! And I was there for that! There have been break-ins all over town, a nice man gets clobbered half to death, and I'm shot at. Are you sure that you and the rest of the Barney Fifes of the LPD can handle it?" Tucker fired back. His temper lost, he shot everything he had. "My friend has been dead over a week now." He pointed to Denise. "Her son deserves to have some kind of progress. Maybe if

Courtney and I were shot and killed you could catch this guy!"

Silence filled the hospital room. Rhonda searched for a hole she could crawl into. Stiles, obviously ready to retaliate, bit his lower lip and walked out of the room not saying a word.

"Tucker, the last thing you need to do is shame yourself," Denise chided with quiet authority. "You're not my son, you're a grown man, and I don't have the right to tell you how to handle your affairs. But that was humiliating, and not for me, for this young lady here. This isn't about Bobby anymore to you. And you'll hate me for saying it, but it's not about your wife, either."

He answered her with more silence.

"This whole thing from start to finish is about you proving whatever it is that you feel you need to show us, your family, the rest of this town. Did you really fly up there to Nebraska for Bobby's sake? Did you chase down that, whatever you call it, record, I don't know, because he meant that much to you? Or, are you so desperate in your sadness and your loneliness that you will go to whatever lengths to prove that you have worth to the rest of us?"

He couldn't think of anything to say. He wanted to badly, but the words dried to dust in his mouth.

"It's so easy to say the things that we've heard a thousand times; here goes, Tucker," she continued. "It's not your fault about Bobby. And I know I'm treading on thin ice as it is, but it's not with your wife, either. I'm not going to tell you everything happens for a reason, hon. I won't pretend to understand any of that, but if you don't believe that it happened for something, some good, you will self-destruct or disappear even further away than my son did in your radio shows and your dolls and your toys and all your things." She grabbed her purse and walked to the door. "I don't have anything else to say."

She eased out the door. It clicked shut behind her.

"I don't have any dolls or toys," he muttered to himself.

Rhonda stood at the foot of the bed still unsure of what to do, or to say. She fumbled in her purse for her phone and pretended to check for text messages that didn't exist.

"So you and the guys flew down for Bobby's funeral," Tucker said devoid of any feeling. "When did you decide this?"

"After you left. Dave couldn't come, but he encouraged the rest of us to get down here. And before you say it, I'm sure that for Lee and Jacob it's driven by the fact that they can say to those in the hobby that they knew the great Bobby Ross."

"What's that supposed to mean? 'The great Bobby Ross?'"

"When you get a chance, you need to check out the bulletin board online for your radio show."

"So the episode played?"

"You better believe it. I listened to it on my laptop in the hotel room. It was amazing."

"I set it up in the cue on the computer," he said. "They let it play on through."

"Everyone there seemed worried about you. At the station, I mean. I went there first thing this morning and they told me what happened. The folks here at the hospital said they wanted to observe you over night."

"And drug me out of my mind."

"I think they wanted you to sleep."

"Are you really here for Bobby's sake?" he asked.

She seemed shocked at the question. "How do you want me to answer that? Do you have any idea what

I'll have to do to pay the loan back just to fly down here?"

He slung his legs over the side of the bed. "Okay, I'm sorry."

"I think that lady out there and that policeman are who you should be apologizing to, not me."

He didn't answer her. He would have time for apologies later. In the corner draped over a chair he found his jeans. Rhonda politely turned around.

A double knock rapped on the door. Courtney slipped into the room. Tucker stopped in mid-pull of his jeans and worked up his best smile.

"Awkward?" she asked, clearly tired out from the previous night's activities, but still trying to tease.

"Rhonda, Courtney, and vice-versa," Tucker said by way of introducing them.

Feeling uncomfortable, Rhonda pulled the door open.

"No, that's okay," Courtney said. "I'm about to go on home and try to get some real rest. I could never sleep very well in hospitals. And not for lack of trying, either."

"I just wanted to say hi, that's all," Rhonda said in way of explanation, but Courtney waved it off.

"Tucker, I had an epiphany in the middle of the night through all the drug-induced sleep I was supposed to get," Courtney said. She crossed to him and helped pull the gown off his shoulders.

"I had a couple of those, too."

"How could all of this—Bobby's murder, the break-ins, and what happened last night—be about just one fifteen minute show?" she asked.

"That's what I was wondering."

"You'd be surprised what people will do with any hobby," Rhonda said. "I've seen collectors do a lot of crazy things."

"Commit murder being one of them?" Courtney asked. "It's one lousy—sorry, no offense—but it's just one—what do you call them—fragment?"

"Yeah, a fragment," Rhonda confirmed.

"You said that a fragment is found every now then, right?" Courtney inquired, directing this at Tucker.

"Sure. Usually the sound quality is poor, but they still appear every once in a while."

"This was never about just one missing fragment," she said.

"Nope. I don't think so."

"Bobby didn't just find one show."

"No, he did not."

"There are some missing shows out there that our man wants to get back in a bad way."

"Shows that Bobby took from him," Tucker said. "And I'm guessing a complete serial or two within the series."

"That makes more sense with it being more than one show," Rhonda agreed.

"Yes, it does," he said. "And I'm going to have to say a big apology or two to see if I can find them."

Tucker couldn't get in to see Mose, but he left word with his family that he was thinking of him. It seemed such a trite thing to say, but he couldn't come up with any better. At least the wound was a blow and not a bullet. He needed to be thankful for anything positive otherwise he would spin out of control like Denise so wisely observed.

"It was never about just one show," he repeated to himself as he officially checked out of the hospital. He exited into a day bursting with sunshine and fresh breezes.

A perfect day to catch a murderer.

On his way home to change clothes, he called Stiles. It went directly to voicemail. Naturally, he thought, he wouldn't blame the detective for refusing to answer his phone seeing Tucker's number on the screen. Anger bred stupidity and he had said a whole lot of stupid to the policeman, who wanted to catch the killer as much as Tucker did.

The beep sounded in his ear prompting for him to leave a message. "I'll save my apology for when I can see you face to face. Do me a favor? I think the money trail is the way to track this down. I'm interested in what Detective Phelps has found with the post office. Give me a call as soon as you can." He hung up while pulling into his driveway.

As quick as he could, he showered the grunge from the night before, ate a sandwich, and checked his e-mail. The *Yesteryear* bulletin board had strings of conversations all buzzing about the new episode. Arguments about its authenticity, the sound quality, and a dozen other topics flooded the site.

He clicked a forwarded message from Courtney marked "Urgent."

"In all the craziness last night I forgot to show you this. See attached. –C."

He opened the attachment, which was an e-mail time-stamped from Sunday night over an hour before he aired the missing episode. The sender ID knotted his stomach. AnthBoucher@AnthBoucher.net displayed in its slot.

"Our mysterious Anthony Boucher," he mumbled.

The e-mail read: "That show is mine, Mr. Niles. They all are. Don't air it. This isn't a warning. – Boucher." Simple, but to the point, the message didn't help his stomach any. Who was Boucher?

Tucker found the Lyle PD website, hit the link to Stiles' e-mail, and forwarded the message with a note explaining how he got it. As he clicked the send button, it occurred to him that he could track the e-mail himself. He remembered a trick Bobby taught him when he wanted to check if a source was legit or not.

He double-clicked the message he had just sent and hit the "Options" button at the top. Finding "Headers," he tapped it, opening up the IP address. He scrolled down searching for the "Received" line of the text. He highlighted the series of numbers separated by periods and hit Control C to copy it. Opening another tab, he clicked "Favorites," and ran the mouse pointer over to the IP Finder address he had bookmarked a few months back. Plugging in the number with a Control V to paste it, Tucker clicked the Enter button.

In less than two seconds, a list of information blipped on the screen. He read through the list quickly: Country: USA, Region: Oklahoma. He ignored the latitude and longitude. He moved further down the screen to find the city of origin: Lyle. That didn't surprise him, but it didn't help his nerves any, either.

He picked up his cell, dug for a phone book in his desk drawer, and thumbed in the yellow pages to the Hotels section. He dialed the first one on the list. After explaining what he wanted, Tucker was put on hold while the receptionist found the manager. The manager informed him in no "uncertain terms" would he confirm the IP address of one of his computers.

Hanging up the phone, he dialed Stiles again. This time he got an answer.

"We've been tracing the money since day one, Tucker," Stiles said without saying hello. "You're telling us how to do a job we already know how to do."

"I know that, but I was looking for cash sales. Do they have a record of Bobby shipping anything else?"

"Phelps isn't hopeful that they can trace him with their security cameras. They're going to try and track him through the receipts."

"That'll take forever," Tucker said. Urgency turned to dread as he contemplated what the killer might be doing at that exact moment. "Did you get the e-mail I sent you?

"I just got it. This just looks like a crank sender to me," he said. Tucker ignored the sarcasm. He knew he had a lot to apologize for, but not right then.

"The sender ID."

"Yes, Anthony Boucher. You told me all about that. I think it's loony. I'm not saying it isn't something to worry about, but I can't use an e-mail."

"What about the IP address?" Tucker asked.

"Actually, it occurred to me, but I'm not taking it seriously," Stiles said not hiding the grudge he felt.

"I traced it myself, Stiles. Whoever sent that e-mail is in Lyle."

"That narrows it down, but not by much."

"Try the hotels." Tucker heard the commotion in the background as Stiles mulled it over.

"I'll get an IT guy on it. Send the IP address over to me and get off the phone and let me do my work."

"Done, and done."

The line went dead. He stuffed the cell phone in his pocket while he lumbered down the hall back into the kitchen to get a bowl of ice cream. He sensed the urgency building as he and the police were tracing threads in different directions.

"It couldn't have been just one show," he said out loud.

Denise pegged his helplessness and blame at the hospital. She had enough wisdom to see through his thinly veiled wall of vanity about his wife and Bobby. He knew she was right about all of it. Courtney was right, too. And Bobby. They all saw things inside him he didn't want to look at or admit were there.

Even if he had done his husbandly duty by getting in their car, it wasn't a guarantee that he and his wife wouldn't have had that crash. And they both could have been killed, or maimed for life, or left as vegetables. The truth, which he couldn't handle most of the time, stared at him and provoked him to lie low, bury himself in a dream world away from the reality of problems, of turmoil, of loss.

Not the mightiest of quests, but his search for Bobby's discovery, and now his killer, in his mind made up for the mistake of his choice with his wife. In Tucker's point of view, it had to, or he would lose all grip on reality. He wouldn't lose the guilt completely, but he understood that if he could just point the police in the right direction, he could feel some sense of worth. And dare he think it? Possibly redemption.

He finished the ice cream with the sad realization that he contemplated the lint in his naval too much.

Even if they found the IP address, it didn't mean they would catch the killer immediately.

And he knew where Tucker lived. The thought made him freeze, listening at every crack of the house, every movement outside his door, and anything else that made noise.

What was he thinking coming to his house?

He hustled back into his study, grabbed his car keys, and shut his computer off. Thinking he had so many more questions to ask, he resisted the urge to call Rhonda, or Dave, or send a Skype request to Julia Appleton.

"It was never about just one show," he said reminding himself yet again.

Looking all around his car to make sure no one lurked in the shadows, Tucker stood at the door until he felt safe to leave. He locked the door behind him and hopped in the front seat of his car. Whipping out of his driveway, he drove aimlessly through the streets of Lyle waiting for a phone call, a great idea to hit him, or divine intervention.

To pass the time, Tucker stuck in an mp3 disc with *I Love a Mystery* on it. A train whistle blasting started the program with an announcer introducing the beginning of the show. Organ music played as screeching tires built in volume underneath it. Both sounds faded out fast with clock chimes marking the time in the action of the show, completing the show's introduction.

Tucker's attention pulled into the dialogue between Jack, Doc, and Reggie trying to figure out how to spend $25,000. Forgetting a destination, Tucker melted into the drama and adventure of the episode.

Considered to be the greatest show ever produced during the golden age of radio, the program did have its allurement. Tucker enjoyed it every time he listened to it, but he couldn't agree that Morse's show was the best radio offered. He leaned toward some of Norman Corwin's work, and naturally the infamous *War of the Worlds* presented by Mercury Theatre on the Air. But who could resist the blood and thunder of three adventurers with no rules, no constraints, and no boundaries?

Bobby's care in keeping his pursuits secret meant he had found more than just a fragment. Tucker kept coming back to that. He pulled the thread from the other end. Robert Bellevue had bought up as many transcription discs of old radio show before collecting really began. He shared, or bragged, to other fans about his vast holdings, but didn't count on the greed of one of them. A party using the "Anthony Boucher" handle supposedly got inside Bellevue's house, figured out a way to thieve some of the discs, and did so. He sat on his stash until the interest in the hobby grew and spread the news that he alone enjoyed missing episodes of the famous show. He also bragged about his thievery. His cutthroat methods earned him the spite of every old-time radio collector out there.

What did he care if one fifteen minute episode, a fragment of an eighteen or twenty episode run, got out to the public? Even today, a fragment here and there appeared on the circuit.

"Bobby stole a run," he said out loud. "That has to be it. He must've gotten a whole series. Why else would he have been killed?"

He turned a corner onto Main Street. Seeing the owner of Hibler Glass walking on the sidewalk, he waved. He nodded at a couple of other folks he knew from either church or at some other business KLMA did business with. It seemed like he knew everyone in this town, where they lived, where they worked, and where they went to church.

The killer knows where I live, he thought. And Bobby, too.

A sick feeling hit him. Whose other addresses does he have?

Ramming the foot feed hard to the floor, he spun around the next corner down a residential street. Not thinking about any pedestrians, he ran stop signs and through lights. He picked up his phone from the seat. He got Stiles' voicemail again. Making it short, he told the detective where to come.

Wishing he'd thought of it earlier, he cursed himself for being on the other end of town from his destination. He drove around a school bus slowing to a stop to let kids out. The blinking stop sign swung out just as he shot in front of it.

Barely missing a car oozing across a four-way, Tucker plowed into a front yard inching past an oak tree and several bushes. He braked, jerked the steering wheel to the left, and got back onto the street. He could hear a horn blaring back behind him.

His cell phone chimed. Someone sent him a text.

"Where RU?" It was from Courtney. He flung the cell back into the passenger's seat. He could call her later.

Pulling up fast behind a slow moving car, he slammed the brakes. His tires squealed with smoke rising up in his rearview mirror. Another car came from the other direction. He eased into a shallow ravine near the Methodist church, passed the car, and hit the accelerator again.

He made the last turn with the streets cleared and nearly slammed his car into the house. Gravel from the driveway flew in all directions when he hit the brakes. Tucker flew out of the car and to the front door. Not bothering to knock he burst inside.

The house had been wrecked. This hadn't been a simple search. Plates, jars, forks, and other cutlery were strewn all over the kitchen. A table rested on its side. The china cabinet lay in shards of glass on the living room floor.

Tucker ran through the house searching for any sign of life. No one was there. He jerked the phone from its cradle, but it had been ripped from the wall. His cell was in the car.

"Not again, not again," he said. "Please don't let this happen."

He became frantic as he ran through the back yard. He looked for neighbors, but didn't see anyone. Not able to tell if they were home or not, he didn't bother running through the neighborhood knocking on doors to find out.

Tucker ran back into the house and searched for another phone. In the master bedroom he saw one on the nightstand. He pressed "9" when a greeting card next to the phone caught his attention. He recognized the handwriting.

Bobby had sent a card to his mother. The envelope was with it. The postage date stamp in red ink had the day before Bobby's death printed clearly next to the return address.

The card had a bunny on it pronouncing some holiday. Tucker ignored the card's message and opened up the card. Underneath the quirky saying, Bobby signed: "I think about our old house all the time. Love, B."

Tucker ran straight out of the house back into his car. He reversed into the street, jerked the gear shift into "drive," and spun out, heading back toward the other end of town where he'd just come from. He dialed Stiles again. This time he answered.

"No time," Tucker exclaimed. "I have another address for you. We need to get there pronto because I think Denise is in danger." He spit out the address and hung up without ceremony.

Shooting across Main Street, he turned onto an unmarked lane where for ages the uppity of Lyle said the "undesirables" lived. Tucker knew that wasn't the word usually spoken, but he didn't have the time to contemplate. A tight-knit community lived here. Each family recognized the plight of the other and formed a bond based on that. Their children wore the threadbare clothes at school. They needed assistance from the government. Their activities in town received scornful looks and even reproach.

And a young Denise Ross grew up here before marrying money and moving out. But as an act of remembrance and grounding, she still owned the house. She used it as a reminder to Bobby about his roots, to give him humility as he spent his inheritance on "silly things."

A car Tucker took to be a rental was in the driveway. He killed his car a block down the street, and without waiting for the police, he hopped out of the car and moved toward the side of the house. He slunk through some bushes planted by the house next door easing up near the front porch. He strained to hear anything, but couldn't.

Scaring him half to death, his cell phone buzzed in his pocket. He hit a button on the side, stopping it and read the text Stiles sent to him. It reported in quick text blurbs that Bobby used cash to ship something big the afternoon before he was killed, which Tucker already had guessed. The rest of the message read: "A. Boucher at Holiday Inn Express."

Feeling a step ahead of the police didn't make him feel any better. Boucher left a trail now, which meant he cared only about one thing: getting those shows back. In the chaos of last night and his determination to keep going, Boucher's connection to the *Sherlock Holmes* radio show bugged him. In the past few days someone told him about a fan of the program, but with everyone he met listing their personal favorites, he couldn't discern who liked what.

Without anyone really knowing what Boucher looked like made it more difficult. Julia Appleton spoke of his arrogance and *braggadocio*. But just like a spider at the center of the web, he kept tabs on everything going on in the hobby. He dug into the network and had a line on everything—his show via the website, Bobby's movements through Rhonda, where he and Bobby lived, Bobby's mother's address, and a score of other things that occurred to Tucker.

The killing couldn't have been him, though, Tucker thought as he eased toward the window overlooking the front porch. Even Detective Phelps admitted that looked all pro, not done by an amateur. The break-ins were another question for another time, if there was going to be another time. But financing the murder and the burglaries would have been no trouble?

Hadn't he boasted about a big sale just a few months back?

Tucker crawled onto the porch, getting splinters of the old wood stuck into his hands for the trouble. Without a curtain, he could peer into the house. Taking a deep breath, he popped his head up and back down just as quick.

He saw Denise standing against the wall of what had been a living room with her arms folded tightly across her chest. Kneeling over a large wooden box, he caught a glimpse of his quarry with a pocketknife about to cut through a woven strap wrapped around the package.

Listening for a siren, or a car, or a sign the police were coming, and hearing nothing, he hesitated on what he should do. He'd driven like a demon to get here to do what? What did he think he could possibly do?

In his memory he heard himself tell his wife that he couldn't be bugged to see her folks on that fateful night. She kissed him goodbye with her warm lips, hugged him close with her loving arms. In his mind's eye he watched Bobby fall to the floor of the hotel bleeding out his life with no one there to help him.

I can't let this happen, he thought. *I won't.*

Seeing the front door open, he galloped through it at full speed hammering into his adversary.

PART FOUR

RADIO GENTLEMEN: THE LIFE AND TIMES OF
TUCKER NILES Episode #25

MUSIC: THEME. WAGNER PIECE.

ANNOUNCER: We return now to *Radio Gentlemen:*
The Life and Times of Tucker Niles.

MUSIC: THEME BUILDS, THEN OUT.

ANNOUNCER: Tucker Niles has run out of time. The
answers found and the killer at bay, he must decide
what is more important—life or taking a stand!

SFX: FOOTSTEPS RUNNING ON CONCRETE.

ANNOUNCER: Will he see another tomorrow?

MUSIC: THEME. SUBDUED/DARK.

SFX: GUN SHOTS FIRING

SFX: A SCREAMING WOMAN

ANNOUNCER: Join us find out…in today's episode
of *Tucker Niles*!

SFX: A CAR DRIVING FAST ON HIGHWAY

TUCKER: (voice over narration) As I ran through the
front door of the lonely, crumbling house, I patted
myself on the back for my bravery, but also felt like an
idiot because I wasn't the guy with the gun…

Chapter Twenty

Without a word of challenge or taunting, Tucker dove headfirst into the awaiting arms of Randy Stark. They landed in a pile against the far wall of the living room area with Denise on the opposite side screaming. The two, not skilled in any hand-to-hand combat, rolled, fussed, bit, and hit whenever an opportunity presented itself.

Randy landed a quick jab with his left against Tucker's right eye. The skin split below his eyelid allowing blood to run down his face. Randy stuck his knee into Tucker's chest and shoved him off. He instantly shot his roly-poly legs underneath him getting himself back on his feet. Tucker couldn't move out of the way quick enough as Randy kicked at his ribs.

Tucker grabbed a foot and twisted, sending Randy back to the floor. Neither one of them knew where the gun fell that Randy had clutched in his fist when the fight began. Tucker rolled back on top of Randy trying to pin his arms to the floor, but pushed his legs down on top of Randy's so he wouldn't propel him off again. Randy spit in his face, whacked him on the side of the head with a fist, and slid out from underneath.

He pushed himself back on his feet again, this time seeing the gun by the far wall. Rushing to get it, Randy didn't sense Tucker rolling on the floor behind him. Tucker kicked a leg into the back of Randy's knee sending him to the floor—yet again. Tucker opened his mouth to yell for Denise to get out of there, but she stood deadly still, seemingly oblivious to the violence in front of her.

As the first words came out of Tucker's mouth, Randy's foot busted him in the side of the jaw. Instead of bracing against it, he turned his head with the blow saving him a broken jawbone. The kick ripped the laceration open more. Blood streamed down the side of his nose, then down his chin to the floor.

The fight turned roughhouse with more biting, spitting, and head butting without the either one giving up. Tucker's blood dripped onto Randy's face nearly sending him into a frenzy. Randy panicked and shoved with the last bit of strength he had. Tucker flew up off of him across the room.

Randy lunged for the gun, had it in his fist, and turned to aim it at Tucker.

Tucker, knowing full well the stakes, grabbed the wooden box and held it precariously above the floor.

The room filled with the gasps of heavy breathing. Denise, still not moving, snapped out of her trance to watch the two men face each other.

"What? No pithy words to tell me how you figured this out, Tucker?" Randy taunted in between breaths. "Isn't this where the hero does that?"

"This isn't a radio show."

"It would make a good one, you know."

"This isn't *I Love a Mystery*, either, Randy. This is as real as it gets."

"Too real, huh? Let's save all the philosophical debate for another day. Put the box down."

"Is it an entire serial?" Tucker asked.

"You better believe it. Your pal Bobby tracked down my holdings and stole from me! From me, no less!" He gestured to himself with the pistol.

"And yet, you stole from Bellevue."

"From his widow, get it right. Bellevue was dead and gone by the time I traced the missing shows. Do you know how long that took me? Once I found the warehouse she used, I broke in and got as much as I wanted. And then I found a stray episode of *I Love a Mystery* that hadn't been heard in over sixty years. I came back to the warehouse and got a full run, which you hold in your hands and a few fragments."

"I guess this is the part where the villain explains the plot?" Tucker asked.

Randy laughed at the idea. "Who's the villain here, Tucker? Aren't we all heroes in our own little journey called life?"

"Were there any more?"

"She must've had the place watched or something because I waited a week or two before I hit it again and everything was gone. She cleared the whole place out. There's a rumor that she's willing the whole lousy collection to Stanford when she croaks," Randy hissed.

"And then they would be available to all of us. That makes you sick, doesn't it?"

Randy aimed the gun at Tucker's chest. "What makes me sick is you not putting the box on the floor."

"Any way this works out, Randy, we all lose here."

Randy cocked his head to the side staring at him. "How's that?"

Tucker lifted the box slowly above his head never taking his eyes from the gun. Randy tightened his grip on the pistol.

"I still shoot you, Tucker. No matter how this plays out."

"But in my version the box goes to the floor busting every one of the transcription discs inside. And you know they will with their age, getting brittle, and from this height. Where do your bragging rights go then?

Denise gets out the door and the police arrive on the scene."

"But you're still dead. Let me remind you of that."

"Believe it or not, Randy, there are a few things in this old world worth dying for. Today, this is one of them. Make up your mind on how you want to play this."

Randy glanced from Denise back to Tucker...and then back on Denise. Tucker read the look on his face, but didn't consider he would take that as an option.

Without another word, Randy slowly changed his aim from Tucker over to Denise. He grinned wickedly at Tucker. His thumb cocked back the hammer. In the distance a siren wailed. It momentarily distracted Randy, which was all Tucker needed.

Dropping the box back down to chest level, Tucker threw it in an arc straight at Randy. Instinct and his love for his precious shows took over. Randy flung the gun in the air, lunged forward, and caught the falling box just inches above the floor.

Leaning with his head over the box, Randy made a perfect target. Tucker kicked him full in the face sending him careening backwards to the floor. He never let go of the box. Even after Tucker retrieved the gun and the police entered the house, Randy still clutched the box with his remaining strength.

Stiles, with a grim expression, cornered Tucker away from the others. "You're an idiot," he said, not hiding his fury. "Don't say a word to me right now. Someone could've been killed here, Tucker."

Tucker wiped at the blood on his cheek. "You're absolutely right. And that's why I came through that door, Adam. It was the only thing left for me to do."

Chapter Twenty-One

The next few days were filled with being interviewed by the police, seeing that Denise recovered from her ordeal, helping her prepare for the funeral, and the funeral itself. By Wednesday, the day they buried Bobby, Tucker ran on fumes. Sleep deprived, hyped up on caffeine, and not eating much made him jittery, and even giddy.

Randy Stark talked. No one was surprised by that seeing that his ego wouldn't allow him to keep his mouth shut. Bobby had gotten wind of him a couple of years back through the Boucher identity. Who else but a fan would use the moniker of a writer best remembered for his radio show writing? When Bobby showed up out of the blue asking about the A-1 Oil and Gas Company, Randy knew he had a problem.

Tucker sickened at the thought that the sale of a lousy comic book funded the hitman Randy hired, which he had apparently found in a magazine aimed at weapons' enthusiasts. The burglar in Lyle was a cousin of Randy's who lived outside of Shawnee, Oklahoma. Both were arrested and charged.

"Bobby stole from me," Randy repeated several times to Stiles. He justified his every act of violence on that fact alone, including hurting Mose when he wouldn't give him the keys to KLMA. Thankfully, Mose was released and recovered comfortable at home.

Detective Phelps found a weapons stash in a shed outside of Trader Book's. She found tear gas canisters of the same make as were found at KLMA. Randy still kept stock from when he ran an Army surplus store. The gun had been purchased legally two years back and Randy had the paperwork in a pocket when arrested.

The Boucher fake IDs and credit card he refused to talk about, which meant he was shielding someone. Why he threw the hitman and his cousin under the bus, but not this person no one ever found out.

Tucker put all of this out of his mind as he entered the church to say farewell to his eccentric friend. The obituary was read by an uncle, the preacher from their church gave the standard lesson on how life is short, prepare for the next one, and then his turn came.

For two days he worked on a speech that would say the right things, comfort with all the right words, but he tore it up. As close as they were, he still didn't know, or even understand everything about Bobby Ross. He kept asking why Bobby made sure he got the fragment show, but sent his mother the box of twenty—a complete serial—without breathing a hint to him. In Bobby's world it made sense, but Tucker could never decipher it. He didn't need to.

He said a few cursory words of thanks and a quick anecdote about Bobby loving old time radio. He pointed a finger at the soundman at the back of the sanctuary. Courtney waved at him from the back.

"I know it won't appeal to everyone here, and maybe it's a bit vain of me, but I wanted to share an episode of Bobby's favorite radio show. I wanted to do this right last Sunday, but couldn't be there in person."

A few chuckled at the reference to the melee at the radio station.

The lights dimmed and the echoes of the *I Love a Mystery* fragment played.

"Goodbye, Bobby," Tucker said into the microphone and sat down.

For the next fifteen minutes no one said anything.

At the graveside, the preacher spoke some final thoughts and the attendants carefully lowered Bobby's casket into the ground. A sense of relief flooded Tucker. It would take time, of course, but at least this part of the grieving had begun.

The crowd dispersed, many of them saying words of comfort to Denise and other relatives. Tucker moved out of the way into the gathering of collectors who already salivated to know who got Bobby's collection and when it would be on the market.

"And yet someone else will own it and someone after that," Rhonda mused.

They walked out of the bubbling discussions about manmade items that didn't have any meaning just then. He nodded to Jacob and Lee who were arguing about the true significance of the fragment episode.

Tucker made Stiles promise not to reveal about the transcription discs found in the box. Tucker would have to figure out what to do with them. That could wait for another day, another time.

Rhonda took his hand as they strolled through the grave stones. "I wish I could say he was mine, you know. As lousy and selfish as that sounds, I wanted to be the one for him."

"I'm sure you were," Tucker assured her. "Think about it? Who did he confide in about his next big find besides me?" Rhonda nodded her head. "Bobby could do the online dating thing, but the real deal scared him, but for him to have spent as much time as he did with you says a lot."

"You think so?"

"Yes, I do. Come on. I know you met her at the hospital, but I want you to visit with someone."

When he left the cemetery, Rhonda and Denise were still talking, holding one another, and sharing tears.

That night Tucker didn't listen to a single old-time radio show.

The next day, he zipped through his morning routine of shower, shave, and cereal at his breakfast bar. Checking his hair in the mirror one final time, he locked up and drove to work. The goofy llama painted on the side of the building never looked better.

"Morning, Tucker," Jackson greeted him as he came through the door. "Got another account for you to take a look at, maybe cut a spot this afternoon?"

"Catch me later."

He nodded at a couple other employees as he walked down the hallway. He knocked on Courtney's door and let himself in.

"Morning," she said.

"Hey you. I wanted to ask you something."

"Ask away."

"How about lunch today? And if you say that you're already going with Jackson somewhere, I'm riding off in the sunset."

"You better get to riding then," she said. Tucker frowned and eased back to the door. "I'm only kidding. I'd like to do lunch."

"I have another question."

"Okay."

"How about lunch tomorrow."

She laughed at him. "Of course."

"And one more thing."

"I'm overwhelmed as it is," she said.

He sat on the edge of her desk and took her hand. "Sit in with me again Sunday night during my show. I promise no tear gas or guns."

"You want me there?"

"You better believe it."

EPILOGUE

RADIO GENTLEMEN: THE LIFE AND TIMES OF TUCKER NILES Episode #25

MUSIC: THEME. WAGNER PIECE.

ANNOUNCER: We return now say goodbye *Radio Gentlemen: The Life and Times of Tucker Niles.*

MUSIC: THEME BUILDS, THEN OUT.

ANNOUNCER: Thank you for listening to *Radio Gentlemen: The Life and Times of Tucker Niles.* And remember the next time you have glass or windows needs, it's Hibler's Glass…guaranteed glass.

SFX: A HAPPY TUNE WHISTLED.

ANNOUNCER: Join us next week for *Radio Gentlemen: The Life and Times of Tucker Niles.*

MUSIC: THEME. LIGHT/AIRY

END OF PROGRAM.

THE END

ABOUT THE AUTHOR

 Bret Jones is the Program Director of Theatre at Wichita State University, Wichita, KS. He is a published novelist and playwright, as well as a film maker. A lover of old-time radio, Bret is the co-founder and writer for The Ancient Radio Players, an audio theatre performance troupe based out of Oklahoma. He has also formed Stagestruck Audio Theatre with WSU Theatre students (http://stagestruckaudiotheatre.podomatic.com/). The group produces audio theatre and has won production awards and been a part of festivals, both national and international. Bret lives in Goddard, KS with his wife, Julie, and their three children: Lauren, Austin, and Emma. http://bretjones.net.